THE TEL AVIV DOSSIER

A NOVEL

LAVIE TIDHAR & NIR YANIV

ChiZine Publications

FIRST EDITION

The Tel Aviv Dossier © 2009 by Lavie Tidhar & Nir Yaniv
Jacket illustration © 2009 by Erik Mohr
All Rights Reserved.

CHIZINE PUBLICATIONS
Toronto, Canada
www.chizinepub.com
savory@rogers.com

Edited by Brett Alexander Savory
Copyedited and proofread by Sandra Kasturi

ISBN 978-0-9809410-5-0

Houses lie, bleached white, along the empty highways.
Pylons jut at angles like bones, the soft black hair of power-lines
obscures the stumps of the phone towers. There is a silence
in the air. No radio, no phone, no television signal penetrate
into that silence. The city lies entombed in sand and sun. The sea
is black with tar. There are no cars. There are no children
playing in the yard. Forgotten laundry flaps on lean-to balconies,
in bathrooms taps run empty, burping air. We are not there.
Where did we go? Beyond, beyond. On top a hill a man looks far
and sees a promise he will not now reach. There are no songs.
We who were there are here no more.

Lior Tirosh, *The Last Days of Tel Aviv*

PART ONE:
PRELIMINARY SKETCHES

**VIOLENT CHANGES,
A DOCUMENTARY (VIDEO RECORDING, PART I—HAGAR)**

I'm standing in the old bus station filming the refugees from Darfur when it happens. The sky turns almost imperceptibly darker, and where before the air was hot and still now a breeze picks up, running against my cheek like a wet tongue, and I taste salt. I am annoyed because I need to take another light reading now and the scene in front of me is shifting, but I have no choice. I am making a new documentary, my third. You might have seen my previous work— *A Closed House*, about that orphanage in Be'er Sheva, or *The Painted Eyes*, about the Russian immigrant prostitutes that I filmed right here in the old bus station of Tel Aviv. I take social issues seriously— I think it's important to bring them to the public's attention, even though it is hard to make a living this way and I still have to work as an usher at the cinema three days a week. I don't mind, at least it's still working with films, and at least I don't have to be a waitress like all the wannabe actresses and singers and dancers in Tel Aviv.

I am here at the station to film the refugees that are smuggled into Israel across the Egyptian border. They're from Darfur, in Sudan, and they came here looking for a place where they won't be killed or tortured or raped. In response, the government locked them up. Our local human rights organizations petitioned the supreme court, which held that the imprisonment was unlawful. Following that, the refugees were abandoned in the streets of Be'er Sheva and elsewhere in the country, and today a group of them was being dumped in Tel Aviv.

While I am filming I can't help notice that the sun seems to dim and the sky is no longer a bright blue but greying and there are streaks of colour running through it, red and black, and clouds are forming in crazy spiral shapes. It is all happening very rapidly. On the ground the refugees are just milling about, looking lost and hopeless, and the few civil rights people waiting for them are handing out sandwiches and trying to see if they can match people to the lists on their clipboards. I hope they can find everyone accommodation. I'd offer too, but I'm sharing a flat with two other people already. Anyway, now almost everyone is looking up too. The wind is picking up and the air feels strange, like there's a raw current of electricity in it. It makes the hairs on my arms stand and I feel sweaty. I point the camera at the sky. Points of light are prickling in the swirling vista of a storm. They look like stars, but—

The wind picks up even more, pushing me, as if it's trying to jerk the camera from my hands. I spin around and the camera pans across the old terminal and someone screams.

I don't know what is happening. The camera is showing the refugees running, though since they don't know where to go they are just shooting off in different directions. There is a low thrumming sound and the earth seems to vibrate. As I turn I see a shawarma stand and there is the sound of an explosion and I think—terrorists. It's a terrorist attack. They always go for the old bus station. The front of the shawarma stand explodes outwards and bricks fly over my head. There are more screams and I am still filming the source of the explosion. The old walls seem to wobble, they move almost like jelly, and something is pushing out of them, vast and incomprehensible, something like glistening air and the smell of salt gets stronger and the wind pushes me and again I almost fall and all the angles suddenly become crazy.

Something, like a column of air, is moving through the bus station, tearing apart buildings, the road, lifting up people. I watch through the camera as a Darfur family gets sucked into the air and shredded—their bits like blood oranges fly in all directions and splatter the ground. I try to run but the maelstrom of air is sucking me towards it, more people are torn apart and I watch an old Chasid in black as he rises in the air and then explodes. There's a rain of blood over the old bus station and the sky darkens further above and the wind moans between the buildings. Another *thing* rises slowly from the ground and then another one and now cars are flying through the air and I see one bus crushed with people inside it, flattened on the road and blood is sipping out through the cracks that are all that's left of the windows. I'm running, I'm holding the camera but it's not pointing anywhere, all I can think of is trying to get away. I weave a path between the things and the wind sucks me once here and once there but as long as I stay in a half-way point I manage not to get sucked in. Everywhere people are screaming and I realize I am screaming too. Something hits me in the face and I try not to look but as it falls I see it, someone's hand, I even notice the wedding ring and the thick black hairs on the knuckles, a man's hand. Is this happening all over the city? Does Iran have a new type of weapon and they've finally used it on us? Is it Hezbollah? Is it Hamas? The Al-Aqsa Martyrs' Brigades? I run as hard as I can, away from the station, without direction. I think the camera is still on.

THE FIREMAN'S GOSPEL,
PART I (ELI—APOCRYPHAL?)

It has been, all in all, a very good day, though it didn't start like one. We rescued a kid who got stuck in a locked bathroom somewhere in Dizengoff street right after beginning our shift, and then spent the rest of the morning sitting in the station, doing nothing except arguing about the proper usage of axes in general and my own axe in particular, a subject upon which Avi and Yekutiel were rather too willing to dwell.

"Couldn't you have at least tried to open the door in some conventional way before chopping it up like that?" Avi said.

"You almost hit that kid's head with it, you crazy bastard," Yekutiel said.

As letting anyone know that I don't give a yesterday's falafel about the life or death of children or anyone else is never a good idea, I didn't bother to reply at all, just applied the old trick of lowering my head and staring at the floor.

"Oh, now you've insulted him, Kuti," Avi said. "I mean, you've got to give it to him, he got the boy out of there in five seconds."

Less than five seconds, thank you very much.

"He almost *scalped* the boy in five seconds," Yekutiel said. "I'm telling you, this guy is dangerous. He has no feelings at all."

I do have feelings. I remember how I felt when I saw the Twin Towers falling, on TV. Or rather, when I saw the firemen working there. I envied them. I wanted to be in their place, every day of my life. Because if there's one feeling I cannot stand it's boredom. I'm an all-action kind of guy. And all I got so far today was this silly kid and a wooden door. I have feelings—strong feelings, you idiot—they're just not like yours.

"Well, just leave it," Avi said. "Is it lunchtime yet?" But it wasn't, and when it finally came it wasn't we who were eating.

"Too early," I said, and just as I was saying it I felt something, a momentary loss of balance, maybe a tremor. "Did you feel that?"

"Oh, so now you *do* feel something!" Kuti said.

"Enough, Kuti," Avi said, and then there was another movement, a rumble, and all of us felt it.

"What the . . . ?" Kuti said.

"An earthquake!"

Israel isn't very big on earthquakes. The minor ones that do occur here are rare enough to be mentioned in the papers. The last serious one happened in the early twentieth century. We're not used to them. We never expect them.

"It can't be an earthquake!" Kuti said, and then, well, it felt as if the whole building went up, then down, and then all the windows broke.

"Holy—!" Kuti said.

"I don't believe . . ." Avi said.

There was a terrific noise outside, that of crashing metal and breaking concrete and the eruption of a water jet, which promptly became visible through our second floor window.

"Holy!" Kuti said.

"We've got to get out of here!" Avi said, the most reasonable thing he'd said all day. We all ran to the firepole, which at that point was already leaning at a rather mischievous angle. Avi slid down first, and I followed immediately after. In the yard, our initial-response fire truck was belly dancing. The other, a Hawk fire truck, however, being heavier and steadier, was only gently moving on its wheels, as if contemplating its response to all this, its long ladder clanking loudly above the din. Pieces of wood and concrete were raining on us, as well as all sorts of equipment—hoses, gas masks, fireproof coats, axes, hammers, cutters and some light pornography. After a while, Kuti also fell down on us. He was never too good with the fire pole. Avi grabbed him and dragged him away. The air smelled funny. Everything looked funny. It was great. And I had just thought of something which could make it even better.

"We've got to get out of here!" Avi said again.

"Wait!" I shouted. "I have a better idea!" And I ran towards the Hawk. Beside it, the smaller fire truck was all but hula-hooping.

"You're crazy!" Avi shouted, but dragged Kuti towards me and the Hawk anyway.

"Get in!" I said, and opened the driver's door and got inside. "We'll get out of here—in style!"

Bless the makers of fire trucks, they never have ignition problems. Avi pushed Kuti into the passenger's seat, and he himself climbed over to the rear standing position. And so, tires screaming, ladders clanking, we drove away from the station, which was, by now, seriously breaking apart—and from the smaller fire truck, which was overturned and blowing water and foam in all directions. The whole thing brought to my mind the history of the old Petach-Tikvah fire station, which burned down twice in less than ten years. What a pity that I wasn't stationed there at the time. But more than anything I was thinking: it's starting to look like a really good day!

THE ORI TRANSCRIPT
(CHAT LOG OF BEN ZIMMERMAN, NYC, NY, USA)

\<BenZ> flight on wednesday, then.

\<Ori> cn't wait 2 see u, bro! i teach you how 2 curse in heb

\<BenZ> you already taught me how to say "ben zona", this is like "son of a bitch" right?

\<Ori> y, but the best is 2 curse in arab

\<BenZ> arab? but they're your enemies, no?

\<Ori> arab's an official lang of israel, like heb and eng

\<BenZ> i didn't know that. so what can you say in arab to piss someone?

\<Ori> say KOOS EMAK

\<BenZ> what's that?

\<Ori> means, the vagina of ur mother

\<BenZ> nice. i'll try to remember that. KOOS EMAK.

\<Ori> wrks every time, remember 2 say KOOS like MOOSE

\<BenZ> koos like moose. i'll remember that.

\<BenZ> so how's the weather in your area? is it hot like a desert? is it summer there now?

\<Ori> spring, lemme go 2 the wndow 2 see, brb

\<BenZ> hello? you still there?

\<Ori> sorry, something weird going on, i dont know

\<BenZ> ?

\<Ori> earthquake or something, dunno, funny stuff in the streets

\<BenZ> what?

\<Ori> ur not going 2 believe it but i think i see a tornado

\<BenZ> WTF?

\<Ori> people are flying, i dont blv it

\<BenZ> you're kidding, right?

\<Ori> i swear! w8, taking my webcam, try to show you

\<BenZ> is this some kind of practical joke? cuz it's not funny.

\<BenZ> you there?

\<BenZ> ori? you there?

<Ori> sory, webcam connected, u c?
<BenZ> no.
<Ori> i put it on the window, u c?
<BenZ> i see something, not sure what it is.
<Ori> people fly! u c people fly!
<BenZ> it can't be. you're doing something! you put your webcam in front of the tv or something, your showing me a movie. i know that trick.
<Ori> i swear its real! ill show u myself in the webcam, see?
<BenZ> i don't buy that. nice try, but it didn't work.
<Ori> KUS EMAK
<BenZ> hey!
<Ori> i swear its real, im telling you, its crazy, i dunno how long i can hold
<BenZ> i'm not that gullible
<Ori> wind like tornado
<BenZ> come on, get off it.
<System Msg: Ori Disconnected and is now offline>
<BenZ> KUS EMAK.

THE MOYSHE FRAGMENT,
AKA THE LUBBAVICHE TESTIMONY (APOCRYPHAL)

They came out of the yeshiva to find the world transformed. They were three: at twenty-seven Moyshe was the oldest. All wore fedora hats. "Does not the Lubbavitche Rebbe say, 'The time of our redemption is nigh'?" Moyshe murmured. There was a scream in the distance, and the wail of a siren, abruptly cut off.

"Long live our master, our teacher and our rabbi, King Messiah for ever and ever!" said Noam, half-singing. He was the youngest, and most recent to the yeshiva. Above their heads the stars seemed to form in crazy patterns. A strong wind blew across the street. There were gun shots in the distance, and more screams.

"But friends," said the third, Daniel, and adjusted his fedora against the wind, "can there not be another interpretation? This is death and destruction all around us!"

"Really, Daniel," Moyshe said. He pulled out a packet of Noblesse cigarettes and tried to extract one, but the wind snatched it from his hand and hurtled it away into the rising darkness. He stared after it with a mournful expression. "Did not the Rebbe's son-in-law say, 'Ask me what I say and I will tell thee that soon it will come true the words *and the dwellers in the earth shall rise and rejoice* and he, the Rebbe, will bring us from exile'?"

"It is true," Daniel admitted. "Why, what then is your opinion of this carnage, Moyshe?"

"Clearly," Moyshe said, "this is the end of days. As had been prophesied so it is. And as you know, when Moshiach comes—"

"Long live our master, our teacher and our rabbi, King Messiah for ever and ever!" said Noam.

"Yes, yes," Moyshe said. "Now, as I was saying—"

A fire truck sped directly at them. A grinning, demented man was sitting behind the wheel. The three yeshiva boys leaped back as the madman drove past them. In the distance they saw a yacht floating in the air, upside down, with its sails dragging on the ground.

"You crazy bastard!" Noam shouted. There was a loud explosion. Soft, warm drops of rain began to fall, staining the three men's heavy black coats.

"I think we should . . . we should go and see if we can help people!" Daniel said. He was surprised when Moyshe, who had assumed a half-crouching position with his hands on his knees and was breathing rather heavily, suddenly straightened up and leaped at him, pinning him against the wall. "Only the righteous shall live, you fool!" he said. "The Messiah is returned to us. What did you expect? This is not Jerusalem! This is Tel Aviv, the city of the shvarts-yor, the city of sin! What do you expect, that God would let the goyim and the non-believers rise alongside us?"

"I'm not sure about this, Moyshe . . . let me go."

Moyshe released him. Daniel massaged his throat. "This is wrong," he said. "I'm sorry. I . . . we must try and help." He didn't wait. Before Moyshe had time to react, Daniel moved. He sprinted down the street, shedding his heavy rekel coat as he ran.

Moyshe stared after him. It took him a moment to gather himself together at this affront. Then—"Ruen zolstu nisht afile in keyver!" he shouted after him, the Yiddish words like poison darts following him. May you find no rest even in the grave!

Beside him, Noam began rocking. "Mosiach," he sang. "Mosiach, mosiach, mosiach, na na nana na. Mosiach, mosiach, mosiach—"

"Oh, shut up," Moyshe said. "Zol dir lign in keyver der eyver!" he shouted after Daniel. May your penis lie in a grave! Noam turned and looked up. "Oh, look," he said. "It's so pretty."

There was a trail of fire in the sky. It looked strangely familiar to Moyshe. It looked like something out of—out of—

The Gulf War, he thought. The first one, he thought. Missiles, he thought. He started to run but there was nowhere to go. He heard the beginning of an explosion; then there was nothing. Nothing at all.

THE LETTER TO THE BROTHER (DIGITAL ARCHIVE RECONSTRUCTION)

Sababi babi babi, my brother! Ahu! How you are? It is some strong shit, man, it is making the ground she shakes! Ahu! Yabba-dabba-dabba! Remember when we were in Lebanon and those fucking Hezbollah shot that missile on the fort and it killed Yossi? It is like this only there is fireworks, very pretty, and Yossi isn't screaming like a girl! I am sitting on the veranda and watching the world go by. You are missing one big fuckin' show here, my man. Remember that model I telling you about, Tali, the one with the big titties? She and a friend came by last night, talking, laughing, smoking some doobie, I put on one of those movies in the TV, a bit of whisky, yaddi-yaddi-yadda, then we make our own movie in my bed. Yeah, man. And then the friend, she is like, biatch, she goes down on me and comes up and she has a piece of paper in her mouth and she kisses me and passes it to me and I says, "What's that, like?" and she says, "It's the good stuff, Mr. Goodstuff," and I'm laughing so hard I mean what the fuck, Mr. Goodstuff? And then I fucked her from behind. Yo.

So this acid is like just kicking in and the girls left and I'm on my own, chillin', thinking about you my brother, so far away in India with the Scandinavian girls all naked on the beach and the full-moon parties and all that shit and I'm making my own full-moon party, why not? Only it's kinda morning, but then the acid is making movie in my head. One movie! It's like *The Wizard of Oz* but in reverse! And all the pretty colours are sucked out of the sky and the world becomes this grey and black and Tel Aviv she is burning and the buildings are collapsing and from up here in the penthouse apartment, with the big cheese daddy gone to LA to schmooze with Milchan and Arad and all the Israeli boys down there in movie-town, I have the whole place to myself, high above the city like a god, brother of mine, like a fucking god. Like, what's his name in that movie with the Ten Commandments. Whatever. Ahu!

There's this things moving through the city, like "This ain't Kansas no more, Tanto," you know what I'm sayin'? Like, what's the English for it hurikan? Huriken?—ah, hurricane, Word spellchecker is my bitch. They're like hurricanes moving through the city and tearing it up and throwing people and cars and tanks around. I think they got your house! I think they got yo mama! OK, my brother, I won't let you down! Maybe I am tripping a little but by god I am an Israeli soldier and I will *not* let the monsters, Arabs or otherwise, ruin this town and take my best buddy's mama and turn her into a tomato sauce. That's it! I'm taking the gun, you know my dad's hunting rifle with the telescopic sight? It's right here, baby! I put the stand up and—here we go! Here we go—!

Bam!

Nailed her baby! Some biatch running around down below and screaming, I mean, a man can't concentrate writing to his best friend, can he? Bam! I always wanted to do that! Bam! I'm shooting those fuckers up, man, I just got someone through the window of his apartment while his scared little face was staring outside—bam! Bam! Bam!

Man, fuck India, fuck *Goa*, this is *it*! I'm like a fuckin' *god* up here, d'you hear me? I'm like James Cameron in *Titanic*. I'm the king of the world!

Hey, one of those tornado-thingies is passing down below. It's pulling into itself like cars and cats and potted plants—hey, it's like a song, my brother—cars and cats and potted plants, cars and cats and potted plants—wo-wo-wo! Easy! The whole building is starting to shake, like, all it's missing is a Kylie Mynogue song, lalala, lala lala la, la la la, and this thing, it's got people inside it and they're spinning, I think they're screaming, I can't even take proper aim, the wind is pulling me, it's trying to grab the laptop, wo-wo-*ho*! My brother, I—

THE FIRST CHILD'S STORY (RANI, APOCRYPHAL)

Shula, our neighbour from the second floor, just flew like Superman out of her window. I saw that because I was looking at the things outside, and she passed right in front of me. I want to fly too, but Mom will shout at me if I try. Last time I tried I was really careful: I had a Spider-Man mask and I invented a special sticky rope just like Spider-Man's webs, only a bit thicker because I took it from the washing lines and put raspberry jam all over it. In the end I sprained my ankle and she was so pissed and I didn't get any allowance for a month. She can be like that sometimes. She says that she has enough trouble as it is, but I don't believe that. I mean, she can do anything she wants, buy anything she wants, eat anything she wants. So she has to work—so what? I can work too. Last summer I worked in the minimarket across the street, packing stuff in nylon bags, got ten shekels an hour. I got enough money to buy a cool model of the Boeing AH-64D Apache Longbow, which is, like, the best attack helicopter *ever*. But of course Mom didn't let me get it. She wants me to save my money. I explained to her that even if I save my money, in the end all I want to do with it is buy the AH-64D model, so why wait?

Everything is shaking, and the walls are making a weird sound. Outside, there are screams. Once I heard Mom scream, when that social worker came to visit. She screamed like crazy then, but when I asked her about it she was very quiet, which frightened me. I used to scream some myself when I was little, but grown-ups are not supposed to do it. Mom said so. And now many grown-ups are screaming outside, in the street. Some of them are flying too, just like our neighbour Shula. Maybe a bit slower. They're very loud. Mom said that if anything happens, if anything scares me, I should call her at work. But I'm not scared. I'm not a baby anymore, I'm the man of the house, that's what grandpa says to me all the time, and I have to protect Mom. Maybe she's in trouble. Maybe there's social workers everywhere, so everybody screams. Mom hates social workers. Maybe they bite you, or sting you, like bees. I once got stung by a bee. I cried for two days—but I was little then. The screams outside don't stop. Mom's at work now. Maybe she got stung by a social worker. I really need the AH-64D—I could fly there and rescue her.

Now there's smoke in the street, a bit like what happened when we put out our Lag-Ba'omer campfire, but cooler, because this one has colours in it. And I hear loud boom and boom and boom, like the thunder that we had in the winter, but I'm not afraid of thunder anymore. I'm a big boy now. I need to find Mom.

I go to my room and wear the blue sweatshirt that I hate but Mom likes, I take my schoolbag and empty it on my bed, then put back only the useful stuff, like the little knife that Mom doesn't know about and some masking tape and some batteries and a poster with the detailed internal design of the Lockheed Martin F16I, which I got from *Aviation Magazine*, because you never know. Everything is moving, and in the kitchen stuff is breaking, so I take my keys and go out and make sure to lock the door because Mom will kill me if I don't. I go down the stairs and out to the street.

There's wind, and there are dirty puddles all around, and some buildings look funny, and there's smoke in colours. There are no people in the street, and nobody's shouting any more. This is a problem, because I thought that maybe someone will help me to get to Mom's work. But there's no one. Then I remember my cell phone. I dig in my schoolbag, hoping that it's still there. Usually I hate it, because Mom insists that I keep it on, and she always calls me just when I'm in the middle of something. Now I think it's a good idea. But the phone doesn't really work—it says there's no reception. I never saw it like that. I hope that Mom's phone has reception, because otherwise she might scream even harder than that other time. Mom just hates it when things break down.

I'm going down the street, to the bus stop. I hope a bus will come and I could ask the driver to take me to Mom. And then I hear something new, and the smoke is going all around itself, and something huge comes out of it.

It's a Boeing AH-64D Apache Longbow!

This is so cool! I saw them only on TV, and in pictures, like in my *Aviation Magazine* and *The Big Book of Planes* and *The Full Combat Helicopter Guide*. It's the Longbow, not the usual AH-64, I can see the difference. Mom can't, but I can. And it's for real!

And it's shooting! Yeah! I think those are Hellfire missiles, and they fly above and I can't see where they're going to hit, somewhere over the buildings. There's a great booming noise, more than thunder, more than anything, and I think I hear a building falling. And then there's smoke coming out of the Longbow . . . no, there's smoke around the Longbow, the smoke with the funny colour, and now the Longbow takes a turn . . . no, maybe something is moving it, like when I play with one of my models, like the one of the McDonnell Douglas F15E Strike Eagle, which is cool but not as cool as the Longbow. Especially the real one. And now the Longbow is on its side and its going down and I feel the wind of the rotor—it's huge!—it's going down right at me, the rotor is coming at my hea—

THE BOOK OF DANIEL,
PART I

For Daniel, running away from the Yeshiva was an affirmation, not a negation. He was relatively newly come to the yeshiva; had grown up outside of Haifa, in an entirely Epicurean household; his grandparents had survived Auschwitz to come away convinced of one thing, which was the absence of God. At the age of sixteen, and following an unhappy, and unfulfilled, love affair and an abortive suicide attempt, he began the process of conversion to Orthodoxy. His parents were unhappy. His grandfather refused to welcome him in his house. But Daniel, with the stubbornness of the young, retained his course.

He abandoned his jeans for pressed black trousers, grew peyes, the long sidelocks of the observant, began attending a boy's yeshiva and studying the Mishna and the Gmara, the two parts of the Talmud, attended prayers, put on teffilin, the long leather straps one wraps around one's arm and head with every morning and evening prayer. In short, the boy Daniel became a miniature Chasid, spending his days in study and his nights in faraway dream lands where the lord God was a compassionate warrior and he, Daniel, his prophet and companion.

Long before that moment on the sidewalk, with the city torn apart before his eyes, Daniel had dreams in which nameless horrors were plotting to seep through and suffuse the waking world. They were shapeless, formless things. They were not evil, nor were they good—they simply did not fit into a Jewish moral framework, or even a generic human one. At the same time, Daniel had dreams of women in various stages of undress which made him wake up sweating, so consequently he did not pay much attention to the first sort of dream.

Seeing the things tearing up the buildings, however, made him remember. Watching as a screaming, terrified child was lifted up into the air, hovered there and then—he tried not to look but couldn't—the child's neck had twisted impossibly and through the torn neck the child's bloody insides were sucked out in slow motion, the intestines like a question mark hovering in the air, each drop of blood like the pip of a pomegranate. The boy was spat out: his empty shell bounced against a wall and came to rest beside his bicycle. Daniel didn't see where his head went. The boy's insides hovered for a moment longer before they, too, were spewed into the street below, forming a shapeless, formless puddle that erased the no-parking lines drawn on the road. How could God allow such things to happen?

He had had doubts; his faith was like a building with weak foundations; it needed constant repair. There were those in the yeshiva who spoke with utmost certainty of the messiah's return. Such a return would herald a new era: no more wars, and peace alone would reign; all Jews would keep the mitzvahs, the commandments of God, and all the goyim would recognise and know the Jewish God. And others still spoke of the End Days, and the time the dead would rise: but it would only be the dead of the Jews, and a few selected goyim, perhaps.

His grandparents believed there was no God. In that they were very much like the Orthodox, for it was belief that powered them. But he, Daniel, did not believe as much as sought belief; did not live so much as dream. And the dream lands which he saw were vast and alien and terrifying places where human faith was a small and inconsequential thing, in a universe which cared nothing for those tiny pinpricks of light in a dark cloth who called themselves people.

He passed through streets that looked like what he saw on CNN—like Beirut looked after the Israeli bombings, like Baghdad looked after the Americans came to visit, like Sarajevo after everyone else in Yugoslavia was finished with it. He ducked between buildings and searched for survivors, but all he could find were corpses. The smell of destruction burned his nose; it was the stench of smoke and rubble and blood and singed flesh. It made him think of his grandfather's stories, of the time he was a boy in the Warsaw Ghetto, running between shelled houses, knowing he only had moments to live.

He wanted to pray, but which prayer? The She'hecheyanu? Blessed are You, Lord our God, king of the universe, who has kept us in life, sustained us, and brought us to this moment?

On second thought, perhaps the Kaddish was more appropriate. He ran, not knowing where, and as he did his fedora hat fell and was snatched by the wind. He raised his hand to his head and, on an impulse he couldn't quite understand pulled off the yarmulke that was there.

Bareheaded before God, Daniel ran.

THE YURI ARCHIVES,
PART I (AUDIO/VIDEO RECORDING)

Dubi is taking too much time setting the scene. We've got to evacuate this cellar in two hours, and he's still stuck in scene three. Rami, the cameraman, is growling under his breath. I'm holding the boom, so I'm being quiet, though I have a bad feeling about this whole thing. Something is wrong, but I don't know what. Amir, who's playing the Golem, is really suffering, because he's wearing this ridiculous cardboard outfit Dubi's girlfriend created. This is probably the most horrible part of being a film studies undergraduate—having to rely on your fellow students' girlfriends, boyfriends, parents and, in at least one case I know of, a grandchild, for all the auxiliaries. For poor Amir, of course, the horrible part is right now, being stuck as such an auxiliary, no doubt melting under the two improvised lamps Dubi got in the flea market after finding out that all the university's lighting equipment was already taken for other students' productions.

The ground shakes. Dubi says, "Did you feel that?"—and then it shakes again. Some of the stuffed animal heads that we put on the wall (all made of plastic, found at a sale in a costume shop) fall down. Dust is coming up through the floor. Dubi says, "Look at this!" and turns to Rami and says, "Shoot it! Shoot the scene just like that! Is the camera rolling?"

"Yeah."

"Sound?"

"Yeah," I say, and raise the boom over Amir's head.

"Amir, remember your part? You're rising out of the ground, flailing your hands, but slowly, right? As if you're in pain. Got it? Scene three take seven, *action!*"

Amir drops to the ground, into the dust, starts rising up with his cardboard-covered hands above his head, feebly moving, rather pathetic. He starts coughing. I get that loud and clear in my earphones.

Dubi shouts "Cut!" and adds, "OK, we'll fix this in editing, let's do another one—" and the ground shakes again, and in my earphones I hear that something is seriously breaking apart.

"There's something wrong," I say.

"Yeah," Dubi says. "The lighting is all wrong. Let's try this again with—" and now there's another sound, a tearing sound, and I can see, not really believing that I'm seeing it, a gap between the wall and the floor.

"Amazing!" Dubi says. "Is the camera rolling? Rami, are you getting this?"

"Yeah," Rami says, and my recorder is running too, and in my earphones all hell is breaking loose. Metaphorically speaking. I'm an atheist.

"What's going on?" Amir says, trying to get out of the cardboard outfit.

"I don't know," Dubi says, and there's that gleam in his eyes, the one like Cameron had when he accepted the Oscar for *Titanic*, "but this film just turned into a documentary. You're still rolling, Rami?"

"Yeah," Rami says. "Keep quiet."

Everything is shaking, everything is turning loose, and I hear wind building up outside. We're in a basement, but I still hear it. Then, suddenly there's no ceiling. The walls are floating, the chairs, the table, the lamps, the camera, we are hovering, and the floor below us rotates slowly. And then I get it.

"It's a tornado!" I shout. "We're flying into a tornado!"

"In Tel Aviv?" Dubi shouts back. "Impossible!"

And as the ground below us rolls, faster and faster, and we take off into the sky, and suddenly I think—it's just like the flying farmhouse in *The Wizard of Oz*; and I can't help wondering where we might land, and whether it'll be in black-and-white or colour.

THE FIREMAN'S GOSPEL,
PART II (ELI—APOCRYPHAL?)

So there I was, driving the Hawk down Ibn Gvirol street, a semi-conscious fireman in the passenger seat and a rather too conscious one somewhere in the back, where I couldn't see him because the right-wing mirror had just been broken by a flying bicycle, rider included. There was a terrific wind, and action all around us, just the way I always imagined it should be. Just the way I wanted it to be. Even better. In some places it looked as if gravity was somehow reversed, cars and trees and people floating up, slowly at first, then accelerating, finally vanishing in some kind of turbulence overshadowing the street. Far in the south, a huge black vertical cloud was visible, and I saw parts of buildings swinging around over that area of the city, as if caught by an invisible carousel. Similar clouds were visible in the east and west, though only just. Around us, people were flying.

"What happened?" Kuti said, waking. "Where are we going?"

I didn't answer. I was smiling like crazy.

"Eli, come on. And where's Avi?"

"He's in the back," I said. I didn't bother even to try to check. Either he was still there, or he wasn't.

"In the . . . oh my God, what the hell is that?" Kuti shouted, and I looked to the right and saw something beautiful: a yacht, huge, flying low and upside down, the stub of its mast digging into the street, rushing straight at us. There were people caught in the remains of its rigging

I said "Wow!" and then it hit us, full force, smashing against the right side of the hawk, making us swerve wildly. After the big crash I felt two minor ones, probably the trailing people. Then I saw the main ladder, which should have been strongly tied to the body of the truck, flying above us right into the side of a building.

Kuti shouted something, but I didn't listen. Somehow we managed not to overturn, and instead did a full circle around our rear-end, sweeping cars over the sidewalks on both sides of the street. The noise was fantastic. Kuti shouted again. I smiled and pressed on the gas pedal.

That was the point at which I understood that everything was different now, that the old rules were gone. That I could actually be myself, and not have to pretend to care.

"What are you doing?" Kuti shouted. "Where are we going? Where's Avi?"

"We're having the time of our lives," I said. "We're going to have some more of it. And Avi is, in all probability, squashed by the Flying Dutchman back there."

"Oh my God! Was he in the rear position? Oh my God! Oh my . . ."

"Everybody dies," I said. It's my favourite R.E.M. misquote, but it doesn't work too good in Hebrew. In Hebrew it sounds just like "Everybody is dead"—which suits me fine, but nobody else, it seems—and the original meaning is lost. Kuti stared at me, shocked by this even more than by everything else. I always thought he was a bit strange.

The Hawk, despite all its weight, including three tonnes of water and I forget how many tonnes of motor and ladders and equipment, not to mention a considerable amount of naval craft remains, moved very fast and very lightly on its wheels. I drove it at full speed through a red traffic light, which looked as if it was struggling to stay connected to the ground. By then we were already near the municipality building, where Prime Minister Rabin had been murdered. The little memorial corner was still there, but numerous parts of the municipality building were gone, as if blown away by an invisible daikaiju not too keen on paying property tax. The road got a little bumpy—some water pipes broke and started spraying water all around it—but the street was clear of cars by now, as most of them were hovering at various heights above it. The roofs of the buildings were being ripped off and tossed here and there. We passed by one of the local McDonald's, which was in ruins, making me particularly happy. Some things should never be called hamburgers. All around and above us windows were breaking, and all sorts of things were being pulled out of them: furniture and animals and people. Everything was flying up. People were flying up. People, like superheroes, free in the air.

For a moment I thought I might enjoy flying myself. Then I saw what happened to those who got too high.

Eventually, all of them got too high.

There was red rain.

It was great to see.

If you looked high enough, there were more reasons to think of hamburgers.

"Kuti," I said, "how about if we stop and grab something to eat?"

But Kuti passed out again.

*

After we passed the point in which Ibn Gvirol becomes Yehuda Halevi street, things went a little slower. The street was narrower, and some cars, instead of flying right up, drifted to the sides of the road and got stuck on walls and in windows, like giant beetles poisoned and put in a collection made of concrete. Pieces fell off them back to the street: mostly doors, but also tires and trunk covers and several whole engines. I drove over all that, but it was getting difficult.

There was no rain here, and it was relatively quiet, though the wind was still quite strong. When I quickly glanced back, I saw several buildings crumble and disintegrate. Before us there was the giant cloud that covered the south part of the city, near Jaffa. Far east and west, other, similar clouds overshadowed the city and the sea. Maybe this place, here in the middle, is like the eye of the storm, I thought. Or maybe it isn't, and whatever this whole thing is, it's going to end soon. But no—I am an optimist by nature. I couldn't bring myself to believe that all this would end so shortly after it began. Not when I was having all this fun.

Kuti woke up again.

"Where are . . ." he said, and then he saw.

"What are . . ." he said, but then probably thought better of it.

"Why are . . ." he said, but halfheartedly.

Then he said, "Stop the truck!"

"No way," I said, and then saw why he said it. In front of us, a pile of rubble which looked like a giant grey turd, but was in fact the remains of a three-storey building, was spread over the road. There was no way that a vehicle the size and weight of the Hawk could cross it.

I said, "We're going to cross it."

"You're crazy!" Kuti said, as I stopped and then put the Hawk into reverse, building some distance between us and the rubble. There was a more-or-less complete collapsed wall lying ahead, like a naturally occurring rump. "Don't do that, don't—!" he added, as I deliberately hit another building, so that most of the yacht went off the Hawk, as well as some ladders and probably the remains of Avi, if anything was left of him. "Let me off! Let me out of here!" he said, as I revved the engine, putting the RPM meter in the red. But by the time he managed to open the door it was too late. I released the brakes, and the Hawk dashed forward, accelerated like no Hawk before it ever had, ran over the collapsed wall and arced through the air. Kuti tried to hold onto my arm but I pushed his hand away from me and he flew out of the cabin and into the sky.

It was rather like that scene in *E.T.*, with the bicycle over the moon, only it was a fire truck and there was no moon. It seemed to last forever. It definitely lasted more than the time it should take any fire truck to return to the ground.

The same couldn't be said for Kuti, though. Again, there was a bit of red rain.

When we got back to the ground, I noticed that the rear part of the Hawk was on fire.

I really couldn't have asked for more.

MINUTES OF THE ISRAELI UFO RESEARCH SOCIETY MEETING, TEL AVIV CHAPTER (AUDIO TRANSCRIPT)

Chairwoman: Shalom everyone. Thanks for coming. First, I want to say thanks to Gilly for letting us use her house again—

Gilly S.: No problem, you're always welcome—

Chairwoman: and to Gilly's husband for the lovely cookies—

Danny M.: I brought the drinks!

Chairwoman: And to Danny for bringing the Diet Coke and the orange juice. Right. Let's start. I'd like to welcome everyone who came—

Misha B.: Aharon asked me to apologize on his behalf, but he couldn't make
it today.

Danny M.: Abducted by the Greys again?

Misha B.: He has an appointment with the doctor.

Misha B.: Why are you laughing?

Chairwoman: Order, please! OK, moving on. First item: the annual payment is almost due. We now have eleven registered members—

Mike L.: Ten.

Chairwoman: Ten?

Mike L.: Gideon's got a job in New York, he's leaving in two weeks.

Chairwoman: Nice of him to tell us.

Mike L.: What do you want from the guy?

Chairwoman: Me? Why? I just think it's basic decency to let your colleagues know if—

Mike L.: I heard you were more than colleagues.

Misha B.: Why are they laughing?

Chairwoman: Order! Order! Mike, I want an apology from you right now!

Mike L.: I'm sorry.

Chairwoman: Right. OK. I want to remind all members to bring the membership fee for the next meeting, cash or cheque. Next week we have a lecture from Dr. Amos Oliani, who is an astrophysicist and has done a lot of research on the Fermi Paradox—

Dganit S.: How?

Chairwoman: What do you mean, how?

Dganit S.: How could he do a lot of research on the Fermi Paradox? The whole point of it is that, though statistically there should be thousands of technological civilizations out there, we can't see any of them, so where are they? That's the paradox.

Chairwoman: So?

Dganit S.: So how can you research something that you can't see?

Danny M.: By watching The X-Files?

Mike L.: Roswell. It's the only way to know for sure.

Dganit S.: Oh, shut up already with Roswell.

Mike L.: Shut up? Don't you tell me to shut up. That's exactly what they want, that people like me would shut up.

Dganit S.: They?

Mike L.: You know exactly what I'm talking about.

Dganit S.: I don't think even you know what you're talking about.

Misha B.: I agree with Mike. The only way to prove it once and for all is for the American military to release the Roswell files—

Dganit S.: You're even worse than he is—

Mike L.: Sceptic! Doubter! Why are you here? Did they put you here to spy?

Chairwoman: Order! Order!

Mike L.: And besides, we all know the Israeli air force shot down a UFO during the Six Day War, and that's what we should be focusing on!

Gilly S.: I have to agree. We need to step up the campaign to have the government release the files of the Tel Aviv Report—

Misha B.: I concur.

Mike L.: Thank you. At least some of us have sense.

Dganit S.: What Tel Aviv Report?

Mike L.: You call yourself a UFO researcher? Did you fall off the ignorant tree hitting every branch on the way down?

Chairwoman: Order! Mike, apologize to Dganit.

Mike L.: I'm sorry.

Dganit S.: It's okay. I'm not bothered by retarded little morons with attention-deficit disorder—

Mike L.: How dare you?

Chairwoman: I said order!

Misha B.: I concur.

Danny M.: The Tel Aviv Report, Dganit, is the top secret document prepared by the special investigative committee after the shooting down of an unidentified flying object over Tel Aviv during the Six Day War.

Dganit S.: If it's top secret, how come you know about it?

Mike L.: I really pity you, you know that?

Danny M.: Let's just say the UFO community has means of obtaining information. Some high-up people in power are sympathetic to our aims, you know?

Misha B.: Really?

Mike L.: Of course. You think Aharon is the only abductee in the country? The military takes the threat of alien infiltration very seriously.

Gilly S.: They say Gideon personally worked with the committee as an advisor—

Dganit S.: Maybe that's why he's leaving the country—

Misha B.: Why are they laughing?

Chairwoman: Order, please.

Misha B.: What's that?

Mike L.: What's what?

Danny M.: I felt that too!

Dganit S.: Me too.

Chairwoman: Dear God.

Misha B.: What?

Danny M.: What?

Chairwoman: The window—look out the window!

Danny M.: I can't see!

Mike L.: Don't push me!

Danny M.: Move out of the way!

Gilly S.: Will you two please shut up?

Misha B.: Is that a UFO?

Mike L.: It's not your standard saucer or cigar-shaped vehicle—

Danny M.: My God! At last! It's true! It's all true!

Dganit S.: It's a fucking car, you idiot—

Mike L.: Oh, yeah—

Dganit S.: Suspended in mid-air by what seems to be a sort of invisible force field—

Gilly S.: And it's moving! But—

Mike L.: It's hostile! All those years, and when we finally make contact—

Misha B.: I think I'm going to be sick.

Gilly S.: We have to stay together. We have to—

Misha B.: Mike! Mike!

Chairwoman: Oh my God. I'm—

Misha B.: Mike!

Danny M.: This can't be happening. This isn't real. This isn't real.

Dganit S.: So now it isn't real? All of a sudden it's not real, Danny?

Chairwoman: Misha, get away from the window!

Danny M.: Misha! Somebody do something! Grab her!

Dganit S.: This thing is amazing! And there's another one! They look just like localized tornadoes, but clearly intelligent—I wonder how they communicate—

Danny M.: You bitch! You heartless bitch! Misha! Misha, I'm coming!

Chairwoman: Bet she heard that one before—

Dganit S.: I'm going out there. I want to try to talk to these creatures.

Chairwoman: What? Dganit—Dganit—come back!

Chairwoman: Shit!

Chairwoman: Gilly, do you have a basement?

Chairwoman: Gilly?

Chairwoman: Oh my God, Gilly—

Chairwoman: The blood—the blood—everywhere—
Chairwoman: I'm going to be sick again—
Chairwoman: Is this thing on?
--- End Transcript ---

THE SHIMSHON FRAGMENT (APOCRYPHAL)

Shimshon sits behind the counter of the bookstore when the first quake shakes the shelves. His rare first edition of *Groteska*, a heavy hardcover by the so-called "Israeli Lovecraft" falls down and he has to get up from his chair to catch it. Shimshon curses and strokes the book's spine. He puts the book behind the counter and sits himself back down and lights another cigarette. What the hell? Earthquakes?

Shimshon returns to his computer screen. The letters dance on the monitor in pretty black on white. He'd written four books so far, and published them himself. Why let someone else handle his babies? Burroughs did the same thing, and for Shimshon, Burroughs is the closest thing to a god. This, his latest book, is going to be the best one yet. *Conch* is about a boy in Tel Aviv discovering a large shell that had come out of the sea. When he blows into it strange things happen. Ancient entities that wear no discernible form rise from the sea and converge on Tel Aviv. The army is helpless against them, and it is left to a small band of survivors to try to escape through the desolate ruins of the city. The hero, named, naturally, after his creator, is called Samson. It is a good biblical name.

There is another tremor and the sound of an explosion outside and Shimshon jumps and the cigarette falls into his coffee and he hardly even notices. A terrorist attack? Another one? This is so bad for business. And rent is so high here on Dizengoff Street. They should never have built so many coffee shops here. It's like an invitation to the goddamned Palestinians to bomb. He doesn't advocate killing them all like some of the extremists do, but really! In the old books in his shop Tarzan had fought the murderous Arabs numerous times. They are like animals. They have no honour. He gets up cautiously and goes to the door. There are no customers in the shop. He hates it when they complain about the smoke. His shop, his rules. Like Tarzan, he is the king of his domain.

What the—? He can't believe it. There's a tank, a goddamned

tank driving down Dizengoff Street. They've really done it this time! They should all be killed like vermin! Bloody Arabs! What the hell happened?

There's a voice coming out of the tank on some sort of amplifier. The voice says: "Stay inside! Lock your doors! Do not panic! The army is dealing with the situation!"

What situation? He runs back to his desk and switches on the radio, but there is nothing but static. *It's Iran!* he thinks. *The bomb!* "I repeat, do not panic!"

Shimshon begins to hyperventilate. Save the book! he thinks. Must . . . make . . . copy. Must . . . backup. There is the sound of another explosion outside and he feels panic rising and his heart is going fast—too fast—and he falls to the floor. What is happening? The book—no, must look first—he crawls towards the door and, through the glass windows he sees the tank, but it is impossible, the tank is rising in the air and—somehow—it's torn, as if it were made of papier-mâché, the cannon coming apart, the tract wheels falling off and the armoured plates crumbling to the floor—it is like watching a butterfly being played with by a child, the way he used to do it, the way—

There are screams outside now. Somehow, they sound to him like the cry of Tarzan, a modulating, loud, piercing sound. He clutches his chest. He can't breathe. Through dimming eyes he sees something impossible—a soldier in the olive-green uniforms of the IDF flying through the air, away from the tank, like Tarzan swinging on the jungle vines, coming straight—

There is the sound of breaking glass, and a hundred small, sharp pains flower in him but he is strangely calm now, detached and very far away. His last thought is of the Jane he never had.

THE FIREMAN'S GOSPEL,
PART III (ELI—APOCRYPHAL?)

The architecture of the south part of the city was wild—at least the parts of it I could see, jumping over the tarmac like crazed kids at an unpopular classmate's birthday party. The fire on the Hawk's tail was growing larger. It seemed an unnatural sort of fire to me. There wasn't so much stuff to burn in the Hawk, it being what it is, and the remains of the yacht should have been cinders by now. But that was logic, which seemed, today, to be on the losing side.

The fire looked wrong, smelled wrong. In fact, it smelled of nothing at all. For a moment I thought that maybe the speed of my driving was pushing the smell away, but I had to slow down several times to cross all sorts of obstacles, and still there was nothing.

I recognized my surroundings as the area of the old central bus station, but only barely. The place had literally been overturned. The ground was covered with smashed vegetables, fruit, fish, ripped T-shirts, broken plastic jewellery and other sorts of cheap merchandise. There were also other things, which, it took me some time to understand, were probably the remains of people. I drove through it all. The vertical cloud was right above me. The air had a funny colour to it, and it was glinting. From somewhere in front of me, an unnatural woosh-woosh-woosh sound was coming, like the wing-flap of an overfed duck.

It was, in fact, a chopper.

It came out of the smoke, rather slowly, not too high above street level. I saw the pilot. He noticed me too. I gave him the thumbs-up, and I think he smiled, though I couldn't see, really, with his helmet on and all. Then his head turned abruptly, looking at turbulence in the smoke to his right. He tried to turn and pull up—I saw his hands moving in the cockpit—but the chopper responded lazily. The turbulence grew and grew, and there was some kind of metallic screech, and suddenly the chopper was covered in shadows. Then something huge came out of the smoke, almost right above it.

It was nothing more unnatural than a flying Merkavah Mark IV tank. I served in the artillery corps, before I was thrown out of the army, so I know. That thing's weight had to be at least sixty tonnes, but it flew gracefully, gun pointing skywards, not hurrying anywhere. Its course was a perfect parabola, which wasn't disturbed in the slightest by smashing into the chopper, which burned, exploded, melted and turned into shrapnel, all in fast-forward. The tank, taking its time, landed on the ground, breaking the tarmac and making the Hawk dance in its place, then sinking into the ground, only the gun remaining above it like a flagpole.

What a wonderful sight! Give me some more of these, and I'd be willing to forgive the army for not letting me drive those tanks myself.

THE YURI ARCHIVES,
PART II (AUDIO/VIDEO RECORDING)

The world is not in black-and-white. It's red. I'm turning around so fast that I can get only vague impressions of what's going on around me. I see people—I believe some of them are our small production crew—but I can't tell who's who. In my hand I still hold the boom, a big microphone attached to a long pole, and I think for a moment that if I was female and just in the right position I could've looked as if I'm a witch riding a broom. But I'm not. I'm flying head-down. I guess it looks stupid. The street "above" looks as if it's about to fall on me, and "below" me there's a pink-red storm. I look at it, over my upward-pointing legs, and see someone shoot into it at incredible speed. Then I feel a wetness. Something is raining over me. Red. Maybe a bit of green. Lumps of something drop on my legs. I have no idea what those could be. I hope.

And then I shoot up myself, my brain pressing against the top of my skull, all my blood going there, the buildings "above" me getting smaller and smaller, the sound of the wind becoming a shriek, the red thing above me pulsating, opening, sucking me inside. Then there's a moment of bright red light, like lightning passing through blood. Then there's noise. Then there's pain.

The ground is shaking, but there is no ground.

The sea rises over the roofs of the city of my soul, flooding it.

And I'm not myself.

An octopod the size of the solar system, pink and dirty yellow like the moons of Saturn, curls around my left pupil, searing it with ochre fire.

My stomach is the burying ground of a lost tribe of minute cannibals. I feel their tiny sharp bones, like hollow microscopic steel needles, shaking inside me, trying to crawl out of their graves.

I cannot be myself. Myself doesn't think in those terms. Myself isn't prone to using metaphors.

I breathe fire. First I inhale it, and it kills everything inside me, billions of sentient microbes the size of elephants, of whose existence I was never aware before, though I suspected all along that there might be something wrong with my lungs.

Who, me?

I see a body, convulsing, shaking, turning inside out, in a red haze. It may be myself. I cannot be sure. I cannot see my face.

Rain clouds are shooting out of my nostrils, emitting short bursts of lightning, smelling of ozone, burning purple holes in the fabric of the universe.

Myself may have taken a drug, it's possible. Myself has done so many times before. But this is unlike any drug experience myself has ever had.

I give birth to a leviathan. The delivery goes very smoothly. The creature flies out of my navel, tiny like a drop of blood, then covers the sky, shadows the ground.

I exhale. Fire.

The sea goes dry, becomes a desert covered with half-caked corpses of fish, black, with the occasional glint of silver. All the deepest abysses can now be seen for what they are, dry holes in the crust of the earth, containing nothing, leading nowhere.

Containing something. Something which dwells underneath the compressed crust of the lowest of the low places of the ocean. Something which lives and dies in darkness, which should never see the light of the sun, or perceive, even, that there *is* a sun. Something that lives upon the tremors at the core of the earth, taking heat and life from molten rock and magnetic resonance and pressure. Something tiny. A dot, a point, a microscopic entity. Something horribly compressed. Something which, were it ever to reach sea level, will be bigger than all the oceans of the earth combined.

Something which notices myself.

The universe explodes.

VIOLENT CHANGES,
A DOCUMENTARY (VIDEO RECORDING, PART II—HAGAR)

I am hiding in the opening of a shawarma shop opposite Rabin Square. I don't know how I got here, all I remember is running, running, and now my legs hurt and my stomach hurts and I can barely breathe but I'm alive: I'm still alive, and I can't say that for other people in Tel Aviv.

The store is abandoned and there is still the smell of roasting meat inside but everything is thrown around. I managed to lower the metal grate over the entrance and now I'm at the window with the camera peeping out. It's been very quiet for a while but that didn't last. The first loud sound I heard—it sounded like back when I was a girl and the first Gulf War was going on and we used to hide in the room with the masking tape on the windows and the wet towel against the gap in the door to stop chemical weapons, and we watched on the television as the missiles were being fired. That's what it sounds like now. Missiles. Someone is shooting at Tel Aviv again, and I have a strange feeling it's not the Iraqis.

The missile attack has been going on for over fifteen minutes. I can hear it, a constant bombardment, the whisper of flight followed by explosions, and I can see buildings coming down in the distance. Sometimes I see people running outside, but they don't seem to have a purpose, they just run, and some of them don't make it. Then I hear a new sound, like heavy vehicles moving on the road, and I look through the camera and there's a convoy of tanks moving down Ibn Gvirol from the direction of the cinematheque. As they come closer I hear a man's amplified voice saying: "Stay inside! Lock your doors! Do not panic! The army is dealing with the situation!"

The situation? All of a sudden I get this huge suspicion and I have to take a deep breath. Is the army responsible for what's going on? Is it some secret weapons programme from the Weizmann Institute that somehow got out of control? Is that what's really happening?

The tanks are coming closer. And then, all at once, it becomes very, very quiet. The bombardment seems to have stopped. I don't see people outside any more. Only the tanks, and more and more of them are coming, and then I see—it's unbelievable—I see this military jeep going past and two army officers sitting inside it and a third soldier with a machine gun at the back, covering them—the officer in the passenger seat looks high ranking, in fact he looks familiar, I pan the camera on him and get a close-up of his face—it's the Aluf Pikud Merkaz, the Major General in charge of Israeli Central Command, and I can't believe it but he's smiling. He has the driver go straight onto the square itself and there the jeep stops and the Aluf gets out—he's got a pistol in one hand and he's smeared his face with battle paint and he's waving the gun in the air and he seems to be shouting but I can't pick up any sound. The tanks are going down Ibn Gvirol and down Frishman and down the side streets, spreading everywhere, and they form an enclosure around Rabin Square. Nothing happens for a while but then I notice Yigal Tomerkin's Holocaust memorial is—I think it's vibrating. At first it's hardly noticeable but then I see the whole frame of it, that massive inverted triangle I remember climbing once during a demonstration in the square. The whole thing is shuddering. The Aluf turns to look at it too, and all the tanks rotate their guns and point at it. The Aluf shouts something, it looks like a challenge, and he waves his pistol in the air again. The Tomerkin structure vibrates harder and then it starts to turn, like a Hanukkah spinning top. It turns faster and faster, and then there's a huge tearing noise and the whole structure lifts in the air, still spinning, and hurtles across the square, above the head of the Aluf Pikud, and into the Tel Aviv municipality office building. All the tanks begin firing simultaneously but there is nothing to fire at. The Holocaust memorial crashes into the municipality building and the whole front caves in, windows explode and rain down glass on the parking lot where Prime Minister Rabin was murdered, and I see the Aluf falling down to the ground and covering his head with his arms and I realize what he'd reminded me of—it was Robert Duvall in *Apocalypse Now*—but he doesn't now, not any more. The spinning Tomerkin structure gets blasted by the tanks and the council building is collapsing and then—

Something weird is happening in the distance. At first I don't notice it because I'm watching what's happening in the square and it isn't good. There is a strong, sudden wind and it smells of the sea and then I see one tank, and then another, lifted up and hurtled about, randomly, crashing into buildings or into each other and one flies over the square and I see the Aluf lying on his back and he is beginning to scream and then the tank falls on him. The remaining two soldiers in the jeep try to start it and somehow they succeed, they're driving through the square while things are flying about them and—they make it—they disappear into a side street and I wish they survive; I wish I was going with them. Then I look up, I think I might be crying, there seems to be a sort of mist and I have to blink a couple of times and—the weird thing—it looks like something is rising in the distance, somewhere near the Dizengoff Center Mall, as if the ground is rising and pushing all the buildings and people and cars and—it looks like a mountain.

NAAMA—PODCAST I (DIGITAL AUDIO)

. . . having said that, please remember that object-oriented programming, despite all its obvious advantages, can be very easily
abused, and that in some cases it might be smart to consider strict
function-oriented design. In my many years as a computer . . . Ahm.
Excuse me. Just clearing my throat. Well. As I said, in my many
years as a computer programmer I've witnessed several such cases,
so I assure you, dear listeners, that this can be, in fact, real. Despite
the fact that . . . ahm. Excuse me. Leonid, please get out of my room.
Later. Not now. I'm busy. No, Leonid, I don't care that you have a
problem. If you were one tenth of the programmer you're supposed
to be you wouldn't have come into my office for a solution. Go read
a manual or something.

Note to self: Delete previous passage in editing.

So, where was I?

Yes.

Such cases, despite being rare, may be worthy of a deeper
examination, as they present the limitations of the most common
programming practice these days. One such case I encountered
while serving as a team leader in Leonid for crying out loud I said *do
not interrupt*! Don't you have any sense of—

No, I don't care if the ground is moving. What ground is moving?
Are you playing again with—

What do you mean "the ground is moving"?

No there's no earthquake. Your hysterics are quite unimpressive.
Close the door behind you and *do not interrupt* or by God I'll have you
fired from this company first thing tomorrow morning. Out. Out!

This Leonid person, unbelievable. I sometimes think he has the
hots for me.

Note to self: Delete previous passage in editing.

So, where was I?

Yes.

One such case I encountered while serving as a team leader in the

IDF involved the conversion of a real-time test engine for a certain kind of radio transmitter/receiver system to a more . . . what was that noise?

Leonid?

What's that noise?

Leonid, where are you?

Where's everyone?

Something weird is happening. I shall continue recording, in order to analyze the proceedings later. There are strange noises from the outside. Looking out of the window, I can see all sorts of things in the street, flying.

This is not possible. People don't fly. Cars don't fly. There must be a simple explanation. Occam's Razor.

It's a hologram. Someone is pulling a stunt on me. They put a sound system near my window, and they're screening images on it somehow. That must be it. I saw that on *Mission Impossible* once. The TV series, obviously. Not the rubbish movie versions. Forget that. Leonid? Leonid! I'm onto you! Stop this foolishness! It's not as if we have too much free time on our hands here.

Maybe it's not Leonid. He doesn't have the guts for it. There must be another explanation.

Ilya?

No, it can't be him. He has the guts, but not the technology. Who, then?

Barak? Rakefet?

Shai? Asaf? Ronen?

Is there anyone left in this office?

Hello?

Now I feel a sort of earthquake. But it can't be. It's impossible. I'm dreaming.

Note to self: Delete previous passage in editing.

But if I'm dreaming there's nothing to delete. Or to edit.

The walls are gone. *The walls are gone!*

I'm in the street. I'm in the air! This can't be real. The only real thing is the MP3 recorder hung around my neck.

Reality check: MP3 stands for "MPEG-1 Audio Layer 3," and is thus a part of the ISO/IEC 11172-3 standard. The first MP3 encoder was created by the Fraunhofer Society in 1994. I'm flying! I'm flying!

My memory seems to be intact. I'm still me. There must be an explanation to all this. I should examine my surroundings.

All is calm. There's no wind. I'm floating in the air. Near me there's a Volkswagen Golf. It's hovering on its side. There's a young man inside it. Now he's flying up through the side window. He's going up in a cloud of glass shreds and plastic. Above him—above everything, now that I think of it—there's something brown and red. It looks a little like a cloud. Not exactly. The young man is now about twenty metres above me. Thirty metres. Now he's in the brown-red thing. Now there's a noise, it seems familiar to me. I can identify almost any noise in the world, if I'm up to it. This sounds just like . . . just like . . . I know! It's a tricky one, because you can't usually hear sounds like that. You have to be able to analyze them, like me. It sounds exactly like a food processor without the noise of its electric motor.

Now there's a wetness. Something is dripping over me. Some kind of fluid. It's as if someone is determined that I reach the conclusion that a young man, above me, was processed into shreds and now his blood is falling all over me. This is, of course, quite illogical. There must be another explanation.

Possible hypothesis: hypnosis?

Possible hypothesis: hallucination?

Make a note of that.

Now I'm starting to move. First I turn around on myself, my legs are getting higher than my head. The MP3 recorder hangs upside-down over my cheek. I hope the recording will turn out OK. Now the whole of me is getting higher. Up and up I go. This means that I'm the next one to be processed. I should be terrified, but this can't really be real. There must be an underlying logic to what I'm seeing and feeling, which will help me to better understand what this can be.

Possible hypothesis: perhaps I was drugged. Question mark.

I'm going up and up. I don't know how long I can stay conscious, hung in the air upside-down like this. Maybe if I lose consciousness this will end. What is going on here?

My feet are now within the brown-red thing above, and the noise starts. No pain, but a sense of something. Something like a hundred million lines of code, all running simultaneously. They feed into my mind. I can see . . . things. Inside. Inside my head. Knowledge! This thing is like a vast computer, a quantum processor of some sort. It . . . analyzes me. It breaks me down into lines of code.

It's a biological processor and, as I'm dragged farther into this gelatinous blob of browns and reds, a little like a food processor too.

Just like a food processor, actually. And I'm the food.

I can't see my feet. A bit of something, some fluid again, sprays over my face. Now my knees are in. My hips. Some more noise. Another spray. My belly. Food processor, under strain. A big drop of something smelly, sewer-like stuff. My chest. More noise, more stuff. My voice, something happened to my voice. My shoulders. The sound becomes a whine. If I had a food processor like that, that'd be the time to turn it off, before it burns up. The noise gets higher and higher, both in amplitude and pitch. It hurts my ears. I hope that my voice can be heard above it.

It stops.

There's silence. Something gets loose. Nothing holds me in the air anymore. I'm falling. I'm rolling in a funny way. I try to look around, but my vision is blurred. I roll around myself too fast . . . like a gyroscope . . . Why is that? I'm spreading . . . spreading my hands and feet in order to be less aerodynamic, create some drag . . . slow myself down . . . It doesn't influence my . . . doesn't help . . .

Ow!

I've landed on the ground.

My head is on the ground.

My nose is on the ground.

I try to push myself up, but nothing happens.

I can't get up.

I'm paralyzed.

I'm rolling a bit. Still on the ground. I'm looking sideways now.

I can't see myself. I can see that my head is on the sidewalk, and there is all sorts of debris around, but I can see nothing that belongs to myself. Nothing. No hands, no legs, no torso.

Either I've become the Invisible Woman, or I'm a head without a body.

Option one is ludicrous. If I'm invisible, my retina would be invisible too, and I wouldn't be seeing anything. Option two is ridiculous. If I'm bodyless, I'm practically dead.

Maybe I'm invisible from the neck down?

No, this is outright nonsense.

There must be an explanation to all this. There *must* be! I must find out what it is. Or die in the process. Or maybe I'm already dead. Or processed. There was something up there, something that saw me, knew me, and for a brief moment . . .

No. Maybe I'm just dreaming. But this doesn't look like any of my dreams. In my dreams I always have absolute control. I've been practising lucid dreaming for years. So where am I? What is this?

I wish Leonid was here now. You always know where you are, with Leonid.

Good old Leonid.

Note to self: Delete previous passage in editing.

THE FIREMAN'S GOSPEL,
PART IV (ELI—APOCRYPHAL?)

All was quiet on the southern front, and I was coming to realize what was disturbing me during this whole otherwise-perfect afternoon. Something was missing. Something very important, which no real action hero like myself can do without.

A soundtrack.

At first I didn't notice this lack because of the tremendous sound effects, the noise made by everything and everybody going up and down and sideways and into each other, all in natural surround sound the kind of which has never been experienced before. But now, sitting in the Hawk's cabin, looking at the remains of the flying tank, it started to dawn on me that the symphony was over and done with and that, except for the background noise of the Hawk muttering to itself on neutral, there was nothing to replace it. It was, all of a sudden, very quiet.

And I needed music.

There was a hi-fi unit in the Hawk, against regulations. I played with the radio a bit, mostly for curiosity, but only got static. A weird kind of static, come to think of it—like whispering waves, with the length of time between each wave becoming longer, and each wave, when it came, bigger than the last—which, to be honest, was better than local radio. I hate local radio. It's all pop and bad Israeli imitations of American rock music and if it's not that, it's "Eastern music," which is what country and folk music is to Americans, only worse. Static was an improvement.

Still.

I looked around for CDs, and found three. Pop, so-called rock. And Alanis Morissette.

The static coming out of the radio began to annoy me, so I turned it off. I felt the adrenaline level in my blood declining, slowly, everything getting more and more relaxed. The quiet after the storm. No! This couldn't be over! Not yet!

And somebody up there liked me, I'm sure, because at that moment I noticed the very low hum, fading in slowly, so slowly, becoming a distant rumble, coming from behind me. The Hawk was still facing south. I opened the door, stood on the last of the three steps leading to the cabin, and turned my head north.

And saw, over the weird flames licking the rear part of the Hawk, something wonderful.

Something grew out of the middle of Tel Aviv. The ground rose. I saw, far as I was, the shapes of sky-scrapers on its top, standing above a huge square building. They were moving slowly, first towards each other, then away. Rising. The whole construction looked familiar, somehow. Then it clicked into place, and I realized that what I was seeing was the Dizengoff Center Mall being pushed up, reluctantly yet steadily, becoming the summit of . . . of a new mountain.

I knew, then, that it wasn't over yet. I also knew that I'd strayed too far south, and that I had to get back to the centre of the city, where the real action was. And in the meantime . . .

I popped Alanis into the CD player. I rolled down the window. I turned the music up high.

"I love the world today!" I shouted out at the sleeping city. "You look good to me, I don't want you to change!"

Tel Aviv didn't reply, and I revved the engine, speeding ahead, crashing into the remains of buildings, of cars, of people, smashing everything in my way.

"You're my bitch!" I sang to my dreaming city. "You're my lover!"

Ahead was the mountain. I hit the gas.

It was then that I heard someone calling my name.

THE TEL AVIV DOSSIER

FIRST EXTRACT FROM THE SHELL LETTERS (INK ON PAPER)

Hiya Nicky, how's it going? Tel Aviv is cool, we left the kibbutz—at last!—two days ago, must confess picking bananas is so *not* my idea of a good time!—and now am chilling on the beach and writing to you. How's London? I heard on the television—we get BBC World at the hostel—that it's snowing? No way! Ha ha ha. Here it's so hot, the sea is blue and calm and I'm thinking about getting an ice cream in a minute—yeah, getting the munchies a little. Jason picked up some local weed yesterday from some guy in a club and, well, you know me, the beach is the best place for it, innit! We're thinking of going to Eilat, it's a city on the Red Sea where it's even hotter—!—and then maybe into the Sinai—that's in Egypt. Duh. Anyway so like everything is pretty cool and we're just gonna backpack for a bit and check it all out, and meanwhile Tel Aviv is fun, had too much beer last night (no change there then!) and it's nice to just lie on the beach and relax.

. . .

Not sure what just happened. The ground kinda *rolled*—you know, like when you shake the duvet or something?—like that. It felt *really* strange. I thought it was an earthquake and shit but the sea didn't move at all, and then it passed, and all the old people that hang around on the beach in the morning just looked at each other and then kinda shrugged. So I figured it was nothing. But—

. . .

Man, Nicky, I don't know what's going on. I guess the best thing to do if there's an earthquake is to stay outside and away from buildings, right? I'm sure I saw that on the Discovery Channel or something, you know what Jason is like with those retarded programmes. Sorry. I know I shouldn't say "retarded" but honestly, all those—

. . .

Shit, something just came out of the water!

It was huge but it had no shape, it was like a massive cone of air, it moved like a corkscrew from the water to the surface and kinda hovered there and if you tried to look at it directly it blocked the sun and also it gave me a headache and I had to turn away. I'm scared. Even the old people look worried. One of them's got a radio and he was listening to some local station, some weird Hebrew music or whatever, and all of a sudden it just stopped, the music, and there was this weird loud static. It almost sounded like a . . . I don't know. Like a *language*, at least if insects had a language. It *definitely* didn't sound like Hebrew, even though the only word I can say in it is "shalom." Oh, and "Ma kore?", which is like a "What's happening!" and "Ken," which is yes, and "Lo," which is no. You don't really need much more than that. Man, I'm feeling a little woozy. I wish I didn't have that spliff now. Anyway, this thing from the water, it—

. . .

OMG! OMG! There were like—I don't know—like three *dozen* of these things kind of, kind of *growing* out of the water, like they were being *born* out of the sea, and they hovered there and then they moved off, they just passed by us, me and all the old people, and into the road and then—I'm scared, Nicky. Do you think earthquakes are like—they're like—*animals*? Like, I know it's something to do with plates and stuff, or is it shelves?—but what if earthquakes were like, well, like *spirits*? You know what I mean? There are these horrible sounds, there are buildings in the city and they're just *collapsing*, and I can hear helicopters in the distance and people screaming, and all the old people look really confused, like they can't decide if they want to run into town or stay right where they are. But I tell you, these things didn't touch us. I vote to stay here. Thank God for this letter, at least, you know, it gives me something to do, to *focus* on, otherwise I don't know what to do—I mean, what about Jason? Shit! I totally, like, forgot about him. He's at the hostel, I mean, is he going to be alright? I thought Israelis were supposed to be good at this sort of thing, like emergency response and stuff, with all those bombings you hear about, but this is just, like, *escalating*, I'm trying not to listen but they are screaming, Nicky, they're *screaming* and I'm scared.

. . .

OK, I'm better now. Sorry about the handwriting. My hands are still a bit shaky. How long have I been here? It feels like a long time's just passed, like when you take an E at a club and all of a sudden it's morning and you're staggering out and your legs ache—you know what I mean? The sky is dark now, and I see stars, but they are like no stars I've ever seen. When I stand with my back to the sea—though I'm scared, I'm scared of doing it!—I can see Tel Aviv, a white city covered in black smoke, and hear the explosions, and the whistle of rockets overhead, though they have almost died out now. It is quiet. There are no more screams. It's like either everyone else is dead, or hiding. Behind me, the sea is a blue-black bruise, I'm—

. . .

Nicky, I just looked out onto the city again and—I don't know how to describe it, just one more crazy thing in a crazy day, maybe—(or maybe I'm just wasted? I hope this is just like a bad trip, or like an acid-flashback like the time we went to the zoo—do you remember? That was horrible)—but as I watched Tel Aviv I saw something growing in the distance, rising slowly over the roofs of the city, and as it grew it toppled buildings and cars—it looks like a mountain. I watched it for a long time. It grew—it grows—over the horizon and already it seems larger than it could possibly be. I don't know if I can explain it. There is a sense of vastness about it, and already it is impossible

LAVIE TIDHAR & NIR YANIV

to see its top, only the lower slopes of it where the remnants of buildings still stand. There's a sort of haze around it. As I watched it I thought how well it fitted in with these strange new stars in the sky. It's growing still, though slower than before. Sometimes I look and I think I see things moving on its lower slopes—nothing I can describe, but giant, shapeless forms that move slowly, with a kind of ancient, patient gait, maybe like caged animals who had been let out at long last from imprisonment—it scares me, Nicky, but at the same time there is something so *awesome*, so majestic about them, that you find it hard to pull away, and when you do the world around you seems less real, somehow meaningless against those distant shadows. I hope Jason will be alright. I'm staying on the beach. Strangely, it feels almost safe here. It's quite crowded now, lots of people came running from the town, and the old folks are still here, and now there are fires and a lot of people talking but mostly it's in Hebrew so I can't understand. It feels—

It feels strangely free, to be standing here, alone in a crowd, on the beach, watching the cold dark stars and their mountain, with my back to the sea. Already London seems like a dream, although I wonder—is this happening there too? And then I wonder if I'll ever find out. I'm going to try and get some food now, Nicky, and will write you more later.

Love,
Shell

THE TESTAMENT OF DGANIT S. (A FRAGMENT)

I hear voices in my head.

I don't think I'm crazy. Or maybe this *is* crazy, I just haven't caught up yet. Or it's the universe that has just gone crazy and *it* hasn't caught up yet.

This is just crazy thinking. I am not imagining this. In fact, I think, deep down, I always knew it would come to this. All those years, the séances, the UFO-sighting trips to the Negev, the telepathy tests, the tarot readings, the meditation, the Tantric yoga, reading Von Daniken, the LSD (but only twice), reading Castaneda (but only once), the mind-group thing we tried in the commune, the nudism, the veganism, the Ouija boards, the Rorschach tests—all that was like basic training in the army, readying me—for this:

The voices are like the babble of water rising from deep under the sea. The voices are like oozing black lava, dripping upwards from underwater vents, burning in the water. Somewhere is another voice, shouting my name. Somewhere far away, in another life, shouting an alien name. Dganit. Dganit. But I am the great nameless. I am a cloud of darkness, a thing which has no name, can have no name, a thing ancient beyond humanity, beyond worlds, a thing not of the world and yet within it. I am naked before it. I spread my arms and twirl with its power, and I speak to it.

It sees me.

All around me they die, humans, tiny things, petals of a rose blowing in the rising storm. Danny and Misha and Mike, screaming but like a weak, soft, final movement of a melody on violin. Violin. Violence. Violated. I feel it through me, like tentacles caressing my body, touching my skin, touching me inside, soft, slippery, sensuous. And yet I know that to *it*, to   , I am nothing, another petal blowing in the wind, and yet—

It sees me.

There is a terrible darkness and I am a fading star suspended in the dome of a crumbling sky. I try to whisper *I love you* and my words go into that horrible, awesome nothingness, but it isn't nothing: it is alive, it knows, it hungers. Words are simply not enough. But they are all I have.

Let me paint you a picture, then, with the words I still have left: Gilly's house broken like a doll's house, as if a giant child had been punching holes in the roof, in the walls, with its tiny giant fists. Gilly nowhere to be seen. Outside, the pavement red and slippery. A 1978 white Toyota lying on its side, the front window smashed, a doll—or perhaps it is a child?—dangling from the rolled-down window of the back seat. Rain falls, and the car is no longer white. Columns of white light, pulsating, growing stronger, swirling like dervishes, their batons people. Someone laughs. I hear the siren of a fire truck. I hear the sound of gunfire. Strange. To hear gunfire. To hear fire. There is fire all around me, alive, a seeing, feeling fire, a cold, indifferent flame awakened from a million years of slumber. Take me! Don't leave me here!

And a part of me, the part that did the degree, and the Masters, the part that was writing a PhD for Professor Amir, the slimy cock with the wandering hands, the cold analytical part of me is thinking:

Some sort of invisible force field, yes. Self-sustainable motion. Resembling a localized tornado. No signs of a biological mind, intelligence might exist on the molecular level, a quantum matrix of probability computing—

And the other part of me knows that these are the gods, the angels, the demons, the monsters of a thousand and one religions made manifest, craving the flesh; and an eye sees me and I see myself in it: an eye the size of a galaxy, with star clouds swirling in its blackest depths, and I, a speck of dust across a universe where I am insignificant, an accident crawling out of a molecular soup, fins becoming hands, a tail growing, falling off, only its bone remaining, a speck of dust daring to stand erect, beginning to think, discovering fire, mathematics, gunpowder, a thinking animal that thinks, mainly, about fucking and, when not fucking, about killing other animals like it. Can you see me? I cry. I scream. I stand on the edge of the road and the road is empty. Take me with you! And it passes me by, and the red rain falls, and the eye withdraws from me, blinks for aeons, turns away, having seen nothing of any significance. Please! I run after the maelstrom. I hear voices in my head, and they crowd everything else away, all thought, all feeling, love or hate or fear, voices alien beyond knowing, voices filling my head to the brim until I scream and scream and scream.

PART TWO:
THE MOUNTAIN

THE BOOK OF DANIEL,
PART II

Bareheaded before God, Daniel ran. Above his head dark clouds gathered, black smoke taking the shape of demons and *ruches*, evil spirits, servants of Ashmedai or Asmodeus, Lord of Demons. When he stopped at last he was surprised at the silence, solemn and profound, disturbed only by the pounding of blood in his head. Yeshiva clothes are heavy and unsuitable for running. He had already taken off his coat. Now, on impulse, he unbuttoned his shirt, and when his fingers fumbled with the buttons he tore it open, and laughed, surprised, and threw the white shirt to the ground. The wind was soft and cool on his chest. More, he thought. And then— more! He took off his undershirt, stained with sweat, and threw it on the ground. More! His shoes! His black shoes! He threw them at a wall. Socks. He smelled them and pulled a face and rolled them into a ball. His feet, sensitive, felt the ground keenly. He kneaded at the asphalt with his toes. It felt warm, and the wind against his feet made him shudder. He stood half-naked in the middle of the street and listened to the silence. Apartment buildings were ruins around him. A broken sign lying on the ground said, *Frishman St.* He turned and turned, spreading his arms, letting the air cool his body. He laughed. Above his head the black clouds parted and he saw the cold immense stars, charting an unknown map in a new sky. More! With shaking fingers he unbuckled his belt. He let his black trousers fall down to his knees, then kicked them off. He remained standing in his white underwear. No more, he thought. The world is ended, and God didn't come. I shall go as Adam did, in the Garden of Eden there on the Euphrates river. I shall go without the leaf of figs, and I shall go without shame.

He hooked his thumbs into the waistband of his underpants and slid them off, and stood naked. He felt hungry then, and he began to walk, treading softly as his feet *felt* every inch of road, every impurity of the surface, so for the first time, it seemed to him, he actually *felt* the city, touched it—so different from before, when he tramped around it with his heavy shoes, like a soldier who feels nothing for his place of conquest, fulfilling a duty, not—-

Not loving, he thought. To touch, to know, was to love, to understand. He never understood that before. He looked at everything with a new light now, as if a scalpel had been applied to his eyes, removing the eyeballs, polishing them, making them new, then returning them gently to their sockets. He saw a teddy bear lying on the ground with one eye missing, and he saw a tank lying on its side, black smoke still rising from its inside, and a soldier lying nearby with his helmet beside him, and one of his eyes running down his face like a tear. He found a fruit stall capsized on a corner, its produce spilled on the ground, and he bent and picked up an apple, and bit into it, and let the juice run down his mouth and he thought—I am alive. The taste of the thought was sweeter than that of the fruit.

He walked, and at last he came to the square of the Kings of

Israel, which later changed its name to Rabin Square, after the prime minister and former general who was assassinated there. There had been no kings in Israel for many years, Daniel thought, a little dazed. And the king who was said to return, our master, our teacher and our rabbi, King Messiah for ever and ever—where was he, now?

The square was silent. Nothing moved. The municipality building lay in ruins, a thing like an upside-down pyramid lying in its rubble. Burned tanks littered the square like dead songbirds. He crossed at the traffic light. He felt, suddenly, overwhelmingly, lonely. They are all dead, he thought. All dead. He missed his friends, there in the midst of desolation: Moyshe, and Noam, and the others in the yeshiva, good boys, really, Moyshe already with two kids and a bright future as a rabbi, Noam trying so hard, a bit slow perhaps but with a good heart, he could have become a true tzaddik, and . . . he wondered if, outside Tel Aviv, things were still normal. He wondered if his grandparents—

Something moved in the distance and Daniel froze. What was it? Ahead of him, across the street and to the left, was a shawarma shop, its shutters closed. Nothing stirred. He took a cautious step, another one—

There! A flash of light! Coming from a, from a—

A small window—it *was* the shawarma shop then. He crossed the road, heading for it. His heart beat fast, the blood rushing through him as if he were running. He came to the place and saw the metal shutter was not closed all the way. Was someone hiding inside? He called out, "Shalom? Shalom?" his own voice sounded thin and insubstantial there in the vast emptiness of the square. "Please, are you there?"

He bent down to pull the shutters up, and when his fingers found purchase for the pull they found something else, too: for when he grasped the edge of the metal someone else's hands were already there. He pulled, and the shutters slowly rose. He heaved at them. The other, on the other side, pulled too. He touched fingers: human, warm. The touch was like a drug. He pulled one last time, his muscles unused to physical labour. The sweat ran down his pale, naked body. The shutters rose. Behind them, standing there and looking at him with a bemused expression on her face, was a young woman.

VIOLENT CHANGES,
A DOCUMENTARY (VIDEO RECORDING, PART III—HAGAR)

For a long time nothing happens. It is quiet, eerily quiet in the square. Tanks are lying lifeless in the street. If there are, as there must be, soldiers trapped inside them, then they must be dead. They must be. Even the sound of the bombings has stopped. From my window I see nothing moving, nothing alive. It is a scene of total devastation, a post-apocalyptic nightmare landscape from a Hollywood movie. But there are no heroes out there. There is no superhuman man with perfect teeth and an indestructible body and a $20-million-a-film salary cheque wandering these streets, the last hopes of a dying humanity pinned on him with the sure knowledge that he would triumph. There is no one here but me, and I am hiding inside a shawarma shop.

. . .

Later. I had to pee and went and did it behind the counter. It was embarrassing, squatting there with my pants down, going on the floor of the shop, but I didn't have much choice. At least it seems safe here. Sitting there in the silence made me think that, almost, life was back to normal. What if I was only confused and somehow ended up in here after my shift at the cinema ended, and fell asleep, and now it was morning and soon someone was going to come by and open the grate and . . . and find me peeing on the floor?

So I did it quickly and went back to the window and put the camera back on. Nothing moving. There are no birds, no cats or dogs, no women pushing prams, no soldiers running late to base, no orthodox debating the *Torah* with waving hands, no rockers, no punks, no Thai or Filipino workers on a break from the construction site or the fields, no wannabe models or singers on their way to Café Joe's morning shift, no retirees with folding chairs and a beach umbrella on their way to the beach, no high-tech executives shouting on flashy high-tech cell phones, no university students heading for a morning matinee at the cinema, no protesters in front of the municipality building, no city council employees sneaking out for a smoke, no joggers, no rubbish collectors, no—

Wait. There *is* something moving out there! Moving slowly, coming from the direction of Dizengoff, along Frishman. Something white and pale and . . . and human.

I can't believe I'm crying. It just feels so silly, to stand here staring out of a window that looks like a small television screen showing a world in black-and-white, the way it did when I was a kid, when there was only one channel and the same things kept repeating until you knew them almost by heart. Like Marco, the kid who'd lost his mother and then had to voyage to find her—why am I thinking this now? And now the figure outside is coming closer and—it's definitely a guy and—

He's naked.

I laugh. I can't help myself. I laugh and the tears drop down my face; I laugh and try to shove my fist in my mouth to stop the sound; I laugh so hard I choke and the tears just won't stop and my body shakes; my body spasms and I can't stop it, can't hold it back.

. . .

Hysterical. I mean, I was hysteric. But I'm fine now. And he's coming closer, I think he must have seen the flash of the camera in the window, and I don't know what to do but suddenly I need to know.

I need to know I'm not alone. I need to know someone else, at least, survived. I need—I need—it's an overwhelming, all-encompassing feeling, a terrible *impatience*, I have to see it, feel it, know it for myself. I go to the shutter and I have to pull it up and I do and—there's something else there. Someone else. His fingers, his hands pulling with me, warm and real. We pull the shutters up together. Light comes into the shop and then the guy is there, and I just stand there and stare at him.

And then he says, "Shalom?"

. . .

I don't want to talk about it. I think the camera was still running when I . . . when we . . . that's just so embarrassing. The truth is, I think I was a little insane when he came through. I felt like he couldn't be real. I had to know. He said, "Shalom?" with this kind of quavering sound, he sounded like a little kid, lost, like Marco in that television program, only he wasn't a little kid, he was a grown-up man and I saw that and I had to—

I just needed to touch him, needed to *know* he's real. I put my hands on his face and felt his skin and his neck and his mouth and I felt his breath against my palms, hot and nervous, and his hair which was kind of greasy and his shoulders, his arms, a little flabby, very pale, like he'd not been in the sun at all. I mean, how do you avoid getting a tan in Tel Aviv? But I wasn't thinking about that then. He smelled sweaty and I just couldn't get enough of it; it was a normal smell, a human smell after the burning and the smoke and hot metal, and when I touched his chest I felt his heart beating fast against my hand, and then I think some of the urgency I felt must have passed on to him and he held me and his hands were in my hair, on my face, on my neck and then we were holding each other and I felt his excitement against me and—

I just hope the camera wasn't running. And now there's this sort of quiet awkwardness, and he says, "My name's Daniel," and extends his hand like for a handshake and I say, "Hagar—nice to meet you," and—

And suddenly we're both laughing, not like I did before, a real laugh, warm and gushing and—and *shared*—and the awkwardness evaporates and when we stop laughing after a long while we just lie back and hold each other. It feels safe in the shawarma shop. And I guess I fall asleep because the next thing I know I wake up and I don't know where I am, and there's the most awful sound outside, like a police or fire-truck siren and, above it, and even worse, a jarring, discordant sound and I don't even understand why or how—somebody's singing.

THE FIREMAN'S GOSPEL,
PART V (ELI—APOCRYPHAL?)

There was nothing in the cabin with me. And it called my name. "Eli," the nothing said. "Eli."

The voice had a familiar quality to it, despite being barely above a whisper. It took me less than a minute to find out that it was coming out of the radio unit. It took me less than five minutes to find the transceiver under all the junk in the cabin, while driving. The thing kept talking, saying my name and nothing more.

I grabbed the receiver. "Hello there!" I said, cheerfully. "How's it going?"

There was no answer.

"Hello!" I said, and suddenly I understood how much less fun it was, to go through all this without having someone to share it with, if only for a short while, before said someone got eaten by red turbulence or hit by a flying tank. It's always good to have someone to talk to. And I thought, maybe on the way to the town centre I can pick up some people. Get myself a bit of stock. Like a puppet show, or the audience in a live-studio sitcom. Who would've believed that something good would come out of mere people?

The radio unit was still quiet, though. Maybe reception was bad. Maybe whoever was calling me had just died, got sucked up into the sky. Maybe I was just imagining things. And then the idea came to me: maybe there are other people, other firemen, listening on this frequency. Maybe there are more survivors, maybe even some like myself—though this, really, was a false hope, since I personally knew all the veteran firemen in the Tel-Aviv-Jaffa area. But hey, what's stopping me from trying to find them anyway?

I took the transceiver. I pressed the "transmit" button. I opened my mouth. Inhaled.

"Goooooood morning, Tel Aviv! This is not a test, this is rock 'n' roll! Come rock it from the river to the Jaffa border, from the sea to Ayalon! This morning—" it was already afternoon, though by the looks of it the time could've been anything between evening and four AM— "we've a wonderful show for you, with storms and monsters, catastrophe and Armageddon, and fun, fun, fun! Guiding you through this crazy time is your favourite DJ, The Incredible Fire-Man, and in the main roles of this action-packed thriller you will find—*yourselves*!"

Then I stopped for a breath and I'm pretty sure I heard the receiver say: "Eli."

Such a short reply for such a long speech. Shame.

"What do you want?" I said. "Who is this?"

Static. A voice too quiet, whispering. Saying . . . "I am the lord your god."

Aha.

"Hey, cool," I said. Maybe there *was* some other survivor like me out there, keeping his senses, most notably his sense of humour. "I kneel before you, O Lord, for I have been having too much fun with all this, which is not appropriate. Anyway, what's your name, dude?"

"I am thy god."

"You bet your skinny ass you are. Funny, we have the same name. Eli."

Silence.

"Don't you speak Hebrew, God? It's the holy tongue, you know. Eli, my God. My God, Eli. You got me?"

Though really it is short for Eliyahu, who the English call Elijah, fuck knows why.

Fine, I decided. There can't be two Elis in this truck. "I'll call you Kishke," I said. "I had a dog named Kishke once. He was a good dog. I hope you can hold up to his standards."

Kishke, from the Yiddish. Meaning kidneys. It's not that I'd ever *enjoyed* eating kishke . . .

Whispering, and static . . .

"Thou shalt be pure in flesh and spirit . . ."

"Though he was, in fact, a very tasty dog. With a bit of garlic, you could almost mistake it for pork."

There was a short silence after this, not even static. God probably doesn't like pork. God is *Jewish*, after all. Then the static returned, slowly, a weak hiss, then an annoyance, like a television tuned to a dead channel, then like a 747 taking off right above your head, right *in* your head, and over it a voice:

"And you shall be my emissary in the desert."

I turned off the radio unit. What desert? This was Tel Aviv. God, it seemed, was clearly delusional.

*

Driving through Ibn-Gvirol Street back north was a lot less fun than going south. It was dreadfully quiet by now: nobody flying, nobody screaming, nobody being chewed by anything. Not any more. No flying yachts either. The real action was to the west, where the Dizengoff Center was still rising, higher and higher. The mountain looked impossibly tall . . . I wondered if, when I climbed it, I could see my house from there. I wanted to turn left and drive towards it, but all the small streets crossing Ibn-Gvirol were blocked by the remains of buildings. They were also becoming notably higher. Ibn Gvirol itself was slowly turning into a part of the mountain's slope, the right side of the street definitely lower than the left. I was concerned that soon it'd become too steep and I wouldn't be able to drive along it without the Hawk overturning. So I continued north, hoping that somewhere near the Rabin Square, the municipality building, there would be an unblocked street which would lead me west and up, let me climb the mountain head-on.

I kept hearing something in my head, like an afterimage of the voice of the so-called God. It kept saying things to me, so weakly that I could understand it only by listening very hard—but I didn't want to listen. After a while I couldn't stand it. I started humming to myself, trying to mask the voice, but it wouldn't go away. I hummed louder, and louder. Nothing. I activated the Hawk's siren.

The sound, through the open window, was horrible, but even then there were remains of talking. My ears were popping, and at some point I noticed I was singing at the top of my voice, no longer Alanis Morissette but a local rock song I'd always hated in particular, but which refused to leave me now. Some band called Ha'Yehudim. The Jews. Dreadful stuff.

So I kept singing and the siren kept accompanying me in time to the beat, such as it was, and this went on for dozens of blocks more until I got to Rabin Square and saw the naked couple.

*

I hit the brakes, killed the siren. My mouth was shut. There was no voice in my head. The two people were getting out of the remains of some food stall or shop, and then they stood on the sidewalk, looking at me. The woman—nice looking, though too pale for my taste—was holding, for some reason, a video camera. The man was even paler. Perverts. They both stared, as if I were something unnatural.

I got out of the cabin, jumped down to the sidewalk. I wore my best smile.

"Hello!" I said. "Having a nice day?" They just stared at me. I tried again. "What are you two lovebirds doing here?"

Both of them looked down, as if in shame. That's one emotion I never understood. It's like feeling bad about something you did—which is crazy to me. But I know shame when I see it on other people.

"Sex, I assume," I said, and the woman blushed all over, which was kind of nice to see, and the man raised his head and looked at me like I was some kind of a rare newt and he was a collector.

"Who are you?" he said.

"My name's Eli. I'm a fireman." *The* fireman. The Incredible Fire-Man! Ha! Why was I being so friendly? I could just run him over with the truck . . . "And you, my man?"

"My name . . ." he looked confused for a moment. "My name's Daniel," he said, but he said it more to the woman than to me, and she blushed again. "I'm Hagar," she said. Clearly I was just getting in the way of true love. Or true sex.

"And I'm out of here," I said. "Have a nice life, as short as it may turn out to be."

I made to climb back into the Hawk when the guy, Daniel, said, "Wait!"

"What do you want?"

"Do you know what's going on?"

"Sure," I said.

"What?"

"It's a *party*," I said, patiently, like talking to a three-year-old. "It's a big, honest-to-God, city-wide festival. You know. Like they had when we were kids."

Then I noticed the woman was pointing the camera at me. I was on film! For real! I said, "Here's looking at you, kid," and then there was a buzz of static, despite the radio unit being turned off, and I said, "Shut up! Shut up already!" and there was a buzzing sound again like someone had just upset a nest of really grumpy bees, and I screamed.

"Are you all right?" Naked Guy, too close, hand on my shoulder. He had a limp dick. It was probably still wet. "Did you hear that?" I asked.

"Hear what?" and then he gave me that look again and said, "You can talk to them?" and he took a step back. Which was good, because I would have punched him otherwise. "Who, man?" I said. "There's nobody here but us chickens."

"What?"

"It's a joke. It's—never mind." Suddenly I felt confused. Static, waves, giant waves, coming nearer, about to crash—I had to get out of there. Go high. I wanted very badly to get to that mountain.

I got back in the Hawk. I slammed the door. I switched on the siren, and the sound was very soothing. I leaned out of the window.

Two naked people, staring up at me, one of them holding a camera. "You'll be glad to know," I told them, "that I've decided not to kill you." I grinned reassuringly and gave them a thumbs-up. I hit the gas, turned right to Frishman Street, which was now more like the Frishman Mountain Road. It went up, not straight to the top of the mountain but close enough. The mountain rose before me. I wondered who those people were. I wondered why I didn't kill them. But it was nice being sociable for a while.

The road was littered with the burnt remains of army uniforms, along with the remains of their occupants, but they weren't a problem, I just drove over them. The road was *also* littered with bombed and broken tanks, and that *did* slow me down. Still, I was close. I switched off the siren. There was static in the silence.

I thought I was beginning to understand what it was saying.

THE BOOK OF DANIEL,
PART III

The word in Daniel's mind was *dybbuk*. It came unbidden. It was something the rabbis in the yeshiva spoke about, sometimes. It was an evil spirit that possessed men. That man in the fire truck, with the bug-crazy eyes and the golem-carved grin that said here was one Rabbi Lowe's Monster who wouldn't shut down voluntarily. Or something to that effect. That was a man possessed. Daniel wanted to stay as far away from that guy as possible.

"This is amazing," Hagar said. She pointed the camera at the fire truck as it travelled slowly up Frishman—literally up. "I am going to follow him."

"You're what?" Daniel saw the rear of the truck find a bump in the road—someone's head. The truck travelled over it, squishing it. Daniel felt sick.

"Daniel!" She gave him a quick kiss, still aiming the camera. "I'm a filmmaker. And this—this horrible *tragedy*, this *unprecedented* disaster, this heartbreaking loss of human life, the selfless sacrifices and acts of unbearable human courage in the face of adversity, this tragic—"

"You already mentioned tragedy once," Daniel said. Hagar sounded like a recital of every Remembrance Day and Holocaust Day speech he'd ever sat through, from kindergarten up. After a while, you got to know the words. Only the order in which they were placed changed:

"Did I? Look up there, Daniel. Look at it!"

He did. Now that they were outside, there was no avoiding it.

The mountain dominated the city.

In the place where the Dizengoff Center—with its elderly armed security guards, its tired sweet shops, its dark cinemas and pretentious mall restaurants and its obligatory McDonald's and two hole-in-the-wall book and magazine shops with their three-for-two bargain tables that never changed—in their place rose a mountain, its peak invisible behind clouds. It gave a sense of enormity, which must have been, Daniel thought, some distortion in the way light passed through the air (he was never much on physics, and the *Torah* was easier), making it appear larger than it was, than it must have been. Yet he could not shake the feeling that there, before him, was a mountain rising to great heights. He swore he saw ice and snow up there. And beyond, the sense of other, even taller peaks: an entire hidden geography, waiting as if it had been there all along . . .

"You can't go there!" he said.

"Can't?"

Too late, Daniel realized he may have made a mistake.

"I *can't*?"

"I didn't—"

"You think just because we *fucked* it gives you the right to tell me what to do?"

He cringed. "I didn't mean . . ." he said, and stopped, at a loss. This was beyond his scope of experience. "What I mean," he said, trying again, but got no further.

"What did you mean, Daniel?"

She looked at him. She was almost his height. He thought she had beautiful eyes, though they looked as cold and as distant as the heights of the mountain at just that moment. And so he did what men had done since the dawn of time in such circumstances. "I'm sorry," Daniel said.

Some of the tension seemed to leave Hagar. "It's all right," she said.

"Just worried," Daniel said. He went to her and clumsily hugged her. She leaned against him. Her cheek against his naked skin, her breath tickling the hairs on his chest. "You don't have to come," she said.

"What? I'm not leaving you—are you really going to follow that crazy bastard?"

"Isn't he fascinating?"

It was certainly not the word he would have used to describe the former member of the Tel Aviv Municipal Fire Department. "Hagar, I don't think we should follow him. I think . . . I don't think he's quite himself."

"I know," she said, surprising him. "You felt it, huh? I have to tell you something, Daniel"—and she nuzzled close to him, began kissing his neck and he felt himself stirring back to life—"I haven't been feeling myself lately, either."

NAAMA—PODCAST II (DIGITAL AUDIO)

My voice sounds weird. I feel nothing below my neck, but there must be something there, otherwise I wouldn't be able to talk, having no lungs. Otherwise, come to think of it, I'd be dead. Or am I dead already? Does it matter? Maybe it's a hallucination—they put something in my food. In my drink, some gas in the air conditioning, some . . .

No. I must be logical about this. I shall describe now what I'm seeing, in the hope that the MP3 recorder is still working—I can't turn it off anyway, under current conditions.

So:

My head is stuck on the pavement and all I see around me is junk and broken cars and broken trees and broken corpses and a little grey dog playing with it all. There's something strange about my point of view—my head is on the ground, everything around me looks huge, but the street itself looks wrong. It looks . . . diagonal. The part of it that I see seems to be much lower than the point in which my head rests. That's illogical—no such places in Tel Aviv. Is this a trick of perspective? Anyway, this could hardly be a drug-induced hallucination, as there's nothing in my life experience to invoke it. I'm not a horror buff; I don't like disaster movies; it just doesn't fit. If it was some drug, I'd probably be fighting a computer come alive.

Or, I must admit, making love to it.

Note to self: Delete previous passage.

Oh, what's the point?

Another reality check: I'll try to call the dog, see whether it responds to my voice.

Hey, dog! Hey, doggie! Hey! Stop playing with that corpse and come here! Come!

Hey doggie doggie doggie!

HEY DOGGIE! HEY HEY!

<quiet>

It heard me!

It's coming around now. It's sniffing the ground, I could almost say suspiciously, but it's slowly getting over here. Come doggie! Come here! Come! Come! Good dog! Good! Goo—Ow!

<panting sounds>

It just licked me. Fuy! Hey, stop it! Leave me! Maybe this wasn't such a good . . . aw! Stop! Leave me alone! Don't push me! Help! Help! Aw! Oooh . . .

<small bark—unidentifiable noises—garbled speech>

Rolling . . . I'm rolling down the street, I'm . . . ohmygodwhat . . .?! Aaaah!

THE FIREMAN'S GOSPEL,
PART VI (ELI—APOCRYPHAL?)

It was love at first sight. The moment the disembodied head flew into my cabin, it fell in love with me. Don't ask me how. Or why.

As for my part, I was innocently driving like crazy up the Frishman recently designated mountain-road, obeying all the rules of traffic I found applicable—i.e., put the pedal to the metal and close your eyes when you feel like it—when I noticed something rolling towards me at tremendous speed. All sorts of stuff was coming down the mountain now—cars and bicycles, twigs, stones, television sets, air conditioning units—but that was slow, and *this* was going as fast as a car. At first I thought it was a basketball that got kicked around by the turmoil, and was ready to pay it the same attention I'd paid to everything else, when it suddenly collided with a piece of debris in the street, jumped in the air like a crazy jack-in-the-box, and was put on a direct collision course with the Hawk. It was then that I noticed it had hair. A disembodied head!

I did the only reasonable thing I could do: I said, "Yeah!" and pressed harder on the gas, thinking of squishing the thing like a bug—on the windshield, if I got lucky, on the radiator grill of the Hawk otherwise.

It only partially worked. I managed to hit it with the windshield, but that didn't get quite the results I expected. There was a wet sound, which I *did* expect, but then it was followed by a sizzling sound and the smell of burning, and smoke *inside* the cabin, and I hadn't quite anticipated that.

The smoke didn't take long to clear out of the cabin. This was in part because most of the right half of the windshield had completely melted. Then I glanced to my right and saw it: the head of a fat woman, brown hair, puffy cheeks, stuck on the passenger seat near me, with something tied around its neck. The mouth was opened in an unnatural way, as if its owner was greatly surprised by dying, which is kind of stupid. The eyes, brown eyes, were open too. It almost looked as if there was still some life in there, as if the eyes were actually looking at me, not just open in a glaze of death. The overall impression wasn't too good, really. One couldn't have failed to notice that this person hadn't been any beauty queen while being alive. Just what I needed: the head of an ugly, dead, fat bitch.

To put it nicely.

Also, the head was emitting an annoying buzzing sound.

Was that a smile on the thin lips of the soon-to-be-skull? Or maybe all skulls smile, even if they've still got flesh on them? And how the hell did it pass through the windshield, melting it in the process? And come to think of it—who gave a shit?

Then I had an idea. I knew what I was going to do. It was just the thing to get me into the right mood.

"Bitch," I said, "you're going to be my basketball!"

I could've sworn the thing blushed.

And then it said, "Hi."

"Oh, come *on*!" I said. "First God talks to me through the radio, now this? I mean, *honestly*!"

"I . . ." the thing said. "I'm, hey . . ."

"If you also claim to be God, I'll be extremely pissed," I said.

"There must be a logical explanation for this," the head said, "but I am—and please do not take this personally—madly in love with you."

Like I never heard *that* one before.

The situation presented a unique opportunity. It could not be said I was entirely averse to female company.

"Will you give me a blowjob?" I said. I was being polite, in asking.

It occurred to me it was a pity the conversation was in Hebrew though. If it was in English, I could've asked it to give me head. Ha ha. Oh well.

"I can't move," the thing sighed, "nor have I ever given a 'blowjob,' but I'd do so gladly if I could, I assure you."

I admit I didn't expect that, but I recovered quickly and played along. "I could grab you, you know, and . . ."

"Oh, please do!"

This was a bit too much.

"Tell me," the thing wheezed. "Is my head all that's left of me?"

"No," I said.

"No?" Sudden hope—eyes opening wide, nostrils widening.

"No," I said. "There's also something tied around your neck."

I gave the head one of my nicest smiles, and moved my hand to grab the something, which looked vaguely like some kind of digital music player. On the way there my hand reached the space in which, this morning, this ex-woman's chest was supposed to be. Then I felt it: something a bit like an electric shock of current just strong enough to make my muscles jump, but warmer, glowing, and with a taste of wind. I looked into the deep brown eyes, and it was all there—the whole world, answers to everything, whatever questions I'd never thought of asking and never dreamt of having answered for me. More importantly—understanding. Togetherness. Union. A kindred spirit. I knew now that this was no coincidence: The head and the Hawk and I were climbing steadily towards something, and it was something wonderful.

Then the Hawk jolted, crashing over a sofa lying in the street, and my hand jerked away, I was quite shocked at what I'd just felt. Crap. Bloody head!

"So," I said. "You know your way in love."

"I . . . I never . . . I never made love."

"Somehow I'm not surprised."

"Will you . . ."

"Look, this is ridiculous," I said. "I must tell you that I preferred God on the radio. It was easier with him." This was not the entire truth, but hey, all's fair in love and war.

"I know you felt it too," the head said. "Some connection, something deeper than just two people meeting by mere chance. There's a reason we've met, I know it."

"Shut up," I said.

"You love me. I can see it in your face."

"Oh yeah?" I said, and with my right hand, careful not to go where I'd gone before, I grabbed the head by the hair and turned it over, so that it was looking into the seat cover.

"Mur muff muffyinf iff," it said.

"What did you say?" I moved it a bit to the left.

"You're just denying it. You're . . ." I moved it back, pushed it harder into the seat.

"Yuff wiff unfefsanf! I fonf finf!"

I noticed the head's voice, muffled as it was, was not lower in volume at all, despite my best efforts, and this discovery was soon followed by another—the voice was now being emitted from the back of the torn neck.

"That's actually a neat trick," I said.

"Muff!"

The Hawk, exploiting the opportunity given to it by the fact that I was concentrating on conversation instead of driving, gently crashed into an overturned, parked van.

"Oh, okay," I turned the head. "Just be quiet about that love thing. You and me . . . whatever love you're feeling, it's not going to work. Trust me on this one." I put the Hawk in reverse, turned the wheel a little to the left, and started forward again.

"I have all the time in the world," said the head. "I can wait."

"For what?"

"For you, silly."

"Stop," I said. "Just . . . stop."

Unattractive brown eyes regarded me and fluttered their eyelashes. It was a little creepy.

"There must be a logical explanation to it," the head said. "I know it. I can feel it."

"You can *feel* that there's a logical explanation?"

"I know it sounds illogical," the head said apologetically, "but it's true. And, given enough time, I shall find the solution. With your help, my love, with your . . ."

"There'll be no time, and no love, and nothing besides it. Look around you. Oh, well, I'll help you look around." I grabbed the head by its hair, turned it left and right. "Look. Do you recognize this?"

"I . . . I think it's Dizengoff Street."

"Exactly. We're now in the Frishman-Dizengoff junction. Do you notice something interesting about Dizengoff? The way that its left side is so much higher than its right?"

"I . . ."

"There's a mountain. And I'm going to turn left now and go up it. That's all."

"And you will take me with you. Together, by the power of our love, we'll . . ."

"Are you listening to yourself, you brainless head? What power? What love? There's nothing. No God in the radio, no love in the air. It's all very simple—I'm a fireman and you're a head. It could never work between us."

"Are you *dumping* me?" the head said.

"In a manner of speaking," I said. Then I lifted it by the hair, put my hand out of the open window, and relaxed my fingers.

The head bounced away.

It was quite satisfying.

NAAMA—PODCAST III (DIGITAL AUDIO)

Love!

I've never felt it before, but I knew it the moment I set foot . . . I set my head . . . I landed inside the truck with the man inside it. And *what* a man! He is everything I have dreamt of, ever, and I . . .

In fact, I don't think I've ever dreamt of a man in my life. I remember my dreams quite vividly, and I'm quite sure that men, in this context, never appeared in them. But this man!

What am I thinking? What happened? I'm not used to . . . I'm not supposed to . . . my God, what a feeling! How did it happen? I remember myself rolling, then flying in the air, then going through something, like glass, but somehow in gaseous form, landing on something soft, then there was a man, and then there was a glow. My mind was like a neon bulb, bathing in short pulses on a low frequency, humming along the 50 hertz of the power supply. Shining, lighting-up, glowing. It took me some time to understand that this was love, but no time at all to know who it was I was loving. He was like . . .

There must be a logical explanation to all this.

I want so much to feel that glow again.

He was like . . . I can't even remember the colour of his wonderful, wonderful eyes. I can't remember what they looked like. What he looked like. I just remember that . . .

I rolled and rolled, after he threw me away, until I stopped on something that I suspect is an overturned trashcan. It doesn't smell good. Luckily, my eyes are turned the right way, south and up, up Dizengoff Street, almost straight to the peak of the mountain. I can see the truck—it's a fire truck, I hadn't noticed that before—driving away from me. I want to shout, to ask the man to come back, but he won't. I know that. I also know that he felt something for me, that there's some kind of unique connection between us. There must be. I think . . . I think I am destined to bring him back.

The truck is becoming hazy now—or am I crying? Are those tears, or is there something, like a cheap special effect, blurring everything? If these are indeed tears, why am I seeing the rest of the street sharp and without distortion?

Note to self: Check this MP3 recording for the voice of the man. In the time it'll take us to meet again, it will be the only memory of him that I have.

Erase the rest of this recording.

*

There's a rumble. Another building coming down. Things roll down the slope. Something hits me, and I fly. Down the hill, away from my man. Round and round and round we go.

VIOLENT CHANGES,
A DOCUMENTARY (VIDEO RECORDING, PART IV—HAGAR)

So we get dressed and there's a bit of awkwardness still there, I mean I don't know what came over me, I don't even know the guy, I've never done anything like this in my life—but then, you have to put it into context, don't you? Extraordinary times and extraordinary measures, who said that? Am I rambling?

So it's a bit awkward but . . . it's kind of nice too. And he wants to hold my hand. Which is disturbing my filming but still . . . it's nice. And strange. But nice. I think. We're going uphill. Everything is at an angle, and here and there there's still the sound of things crashing, buildings falling down, the noise startling in the quiet. Occasionally something comes rolling down the slope—loose fencing, car tires, an Uzi, a potted plant, a dead cat, a frying pan, an old issue of Penthouse, a black Chasid's hat looking like a flying saucer, a dirty-laundry basket made of bamboo, a paperback Amos Oz novel, a TV remote control, a goldfish, a photocopier rolling like a boulder, a Coca-Cola sign, burger wrappers, a door, a little clay figure of the sort school kids make in art class . . . Daniel reaches out for that last one. It's an ugly thing, a grotesque little figure like some sort of primitive fetish figurine, but painted in garish gouache colours. It's a head. It looks like a toad. I almost expect it to blink. I hate toads. Frogs too. Daniel says, "It's a head."

"Yes," I say, a little testily, "I can see that."

"No," he says. "It's a *head*."

"Daniel, I already *told* you—"

"Hagar—"

"Dan—"

I finally look up. And there's a human head coming down the slope towards us. It's disgusting. I make sure the camera captures it. The head bounces and rolls and comes to land at Daniel's feet. I think I'm going to be sick.

"I *told* you," he says.

I *hate* when people say that.

"I hate when people say that!" the head says. "Oh, no, please don't—"

But I'm sick all over it.

"You *bitch*," the head says. I blink back tears. The head looks fuzzy through them. My sick is woven through her thin, mousy-brown hair. It's a fat-looking head. Brown eyes stare up at me accusingly. "Are you going to clean me or what?"

"Daniel," I say, and I can't help notice the note of hysteria creeping into my voice, "I'm not touching this thing."

"What do you want me to do?" he says, all calm, and I could kiss him. "Get rid of it," I say.

"It? It?" the head says. "I'm a *person*, not an *it*. Well." It seems to reconsider. "Half a person?" it says hopefully. Daniel picks her up by the hair. "Hey, watch it!"

"Are you filming?" he says, and then, "Hagar, put yourself together! Are you *filming*?"

And I think, *of course*, and I take a deep breath, and I'm myself again, a professional, and this is work, nothing more. I've seen worse. I point the camera at the head dangling from Daniel's arm. "What's your name?" I say.

"Oho, so you've decided to be polite now?" The head looks at the camera. "I do appreciate it, though. You don't know what it's like, being a head. And I'm not *disembodied*, thank you very much. I prefer body-challenged."

"She is certainly that," Daniel says, and sniggers, but neither of us pay him much attention. "My name," the head says, "is Naama. Allow me to introduce myself properly. Let me see. Where to start. Well, I obtained my master's degree from Oxford University back in—" The head blinks and stops. "But that doesn't matter!" she says. "Forget about me. Did you see him?" There is something lonely and desperate in her voice. I say, "Who?"

"Him! The man in the truck! We—" The head blushes, and her eyes blink rapidly, and for a moment I think I'm going to be sick again. "Turn me around!" the head says. "I have to see him!"

And I know who she means. As much as I don't want to. And I say, "I think we lost him a while back, Naama—" Then Daniel does this motion with his head, this sort of "look up" thing, and he twists the head to face the rising mountain, and by instinct I move the camera with him and there's the fire truck, with that, that *man* inside it, with his head poking out of the window, and—

The fire truck, burning, is slowly rising in the air.

THE FIREMAN'S GOSPEL,
PART VII (ELI—APOCRYPHAL?)

I never suspected there was a direct correlation between height above sea level and all-in weirdness. Not much chance of getting high in flatland Tel Aviv. Not without drugs, anyway.

At first the Hawk and I just went, not too fast but steadily, over everything in our way. We merrily squashed through what looked like the entire content of a butcher shop, the tires making nice sucking noises over the ludicrous amount of raw beef. No matter, I bet it was kosher anyway—and I prefer my food to be free of the tyranny of religion. Then we went through one of those little Cafés that litter Dizengoff Street, and it was all sloshy and bubbly, and I was enjoying the thought of meat mixing with milk on the Hawk's tires. This was all pretty normal.

Then there was the tourist bus. It was green, heavy, and looked brand new. It was stuck vertically in the road's asphalt, standing on its grille, like a pencil shoved into a belly button. I saw, despite its darkened windows, some people crawling inside it.

I didn't slow down. I went right at it, anticipating a nice audio-visual effect when it fell. I was more disappointed than annoyed when the Hawk and myself went right through it without making a sound.

I stopped. I looked back. The Hawk's rear part was still burning quietly, though the flames looked closer to the cabin now. This was somehow reassuring.

In the background of the relative silence, I now noticed the return of the static. I looked at the radio unit, which appeared to be on, despite me remembering distinctly that I shut it off.

"Oh, God," I said. "Not again."

"I am thy . . ."

"Shut up."

There was a second of quiet. Then the static whispered something like, "Put thy hand upon thy bosom."

"So now you're in love with me too?"

"And it shall come to pass, if they will not believe thee, neither hearken to the voice of the first sign . . ."

"So all this is a *sign* now? I don't buy that. I don't buy *you*," I said. "Ciao," I added, and moved my right hand to gently squeeze the power button off.

I touched it, and the static was cut off for a second, then returned at full volume, and the world boomed out of existence and into something else.

The cabin was in flames. I was in flames. They smelled cold and tasted yellow and were bittersweet in my ears, like cheap red Chinese sauce. I still sat in the Hawk's cabin, but not on the seat. Instead, I hovered in the air, my head touching the ceiling. Out of the windshield I saw only flames, and a red-red sky.

I looked sideways, and saw the world turning slowly around me. Below me. I saw the top of the mountain now, the ruined Dizengoff Center, from above. The Hawk was flying.

"Thy hand upon thy bosom . . ." said the static, and suddenly the Hawk jolted crazily forward, upwards, accelerating, crashing me into the seat.

In the haze of blood going to my head, just before losing consciousness, I remember just one thought:

This God person is actually *real*?

THE BOOK OF DANIEL,
PART IV

Daniel dropped the head. He didn't even notice. He was staring at the burning, rising truck. It hovered impossibly in the air before shooting upwards, up and up and up, becoming a speck of dust against the mountain.

"Do you mind?" a voice said. Daniel looked down. "Shit, I'm sorry—" he said. Then he looked again.

The head hovered above the ground. "What—?" Daniel said.

The head looked confused. Then it twirled around. "It's *him*," the head said.

"What?"

The head stopped and stared at Daniel. Brown eyes, podgy face. A spot under her chin. Quite unattractive. "I know," the head said.

"You know what?" Daniel could no longer see the truck. He had a sense of acute *wrongness*. The mountain seemed to expand around them, to fill up the world.

"I know," the head said. It sounded just a little bit smug. "I understand now."

"What?" Daniel yelled.

"Everything," the head said—quietly, with immense dignity. "I understand it all, now."

"At least that makes one of us," Daniel said. The head turned 360 degrees and came back to look at him. "I pity you," it said.

Daniel grabbed the head by the hair and spun around and around. The head yelled, "Hey, what the *fuck* do you think you're doing!?"— and Daniel let go, releasing the head.

"Daniel, what the fuck are you doing?" Hagar shouted. He ignored her and watched the head arc through the air, a beautiful, entirely *satisfying* sight, tracing a curve over the steep slope of the mountain until it connected with the ground far below, bounced, sailed through the air again, bounced a second time, rolled, and finally disappeared from view. He still had the strange child's clay-thing, he realized. And it resembled the head too closely for his liking. He let it go. It fell at his feet and rolled away. Somehow, it made him feel clean. Purified. "Are you *nuts*?"

"Just cut it in editing," he said, and he laughed. He felt like something was laughing through him.

"Daniel, please stop."

But he couldn't. The laughter wouldn't go. It grew, it burst out of him, it shook his whole body, shook the ground he was standing on, shook the—

"Daniel, the ground!" She grabbed his hand. Her touch sobered him. The ground shook. Coming at them down the slope were the remnants of the Dizengoff Center. "We have to run."

"Run where?" he shouted.

"We can't go back," Hagar said. Just then something came at them down the slope, crashed into Hagar, and took with it her camera. She screamed.

"Hagar, no!"

"I have to get it back!"

He grabbed her and pulled her after him. "We could die!" he shouted. Above their heads, thunder like distant explosions was coming near. Lightning flashed.

"Everyone else is *already* dead!" Hagar said, and stopped.

He pulled harder, ran up the slope, pulling her. "But we're not! Come on!"

She followed him. Around them, the remnants of the city centre were falling down, crashing, rolling, as if the mountain was shaking the last foreign elements off its side. They ran through a storm of bricks and glass and people and a poster of *Independence Day* and two flying turtles from what must have been a pet store, past mobile phones and notebooks and oranges that came at them like grenades, past handbags and Italian shoes and combs and a set of false teeth and a McDonald's sign that nearly took their heads off. Above them the sky darkened and lightning flashed and where it hit there was a burning smell, and the thunder echoed around them and the rain came, washing away the city, a downpour that silenced everything and they struggled uphill, running, crawling, falling in the mud, like two insects climbing an elephant's back, and when they couldn't go any longer they fell on the ground and lay there, holding each other, while the rain fell and fell and fell.

*

When Daniel awoke, the city was gone. They were on a high plateau, and above their heads a multitude of stars shone cold and bright and unknown. The peaks of other, distant mountains were just visible in the distance, dusted with snow. There was no city. There was no Tel Aviv, no seafront promenade, no yeshiva and no rabbis, no restaurants, kosher or otherwise, no orange-juice sellers, no girls in denim shorts, no cell phones ringing, no—

No sound, in fact. The world was silent. The world was laid out around Daniel like an unknown map. Somewhere there were seas and islands and volcanoes, waterfalls and valleys and chasms, deserts and jungles and living things . . . living things. He touched Hagar's shoulder, gently, and she opened her eyes. She stared up at the sky for a long time.

When she rose it was with a new silence, and it was echoed in Daniel. It was a silence like an abyss, deep and profound, a silence belonging to this new world, not the old. They held each other's hands. The map of the world stretched out before them, full of blank spaces. Unknown. They linked their fingers. They didn't speak, but they knew each other's mind. They took a step, and then another, and another. Above their heads the stars stared down, mute and strange and old.

PART THREE:
ONE YEAR LATER

MORDECHAI: ONE

I have uncovered and decrypted the secret writings of the Kinneret cult, which was active near the Sea of Galilee since about 300 BC until well after the time of Christ, and had more to do with the latter's performance than the New Testament would care to admit. I have located the hidden cave in which the actual miracle of the container of oil had occurred, the one celebrated to this day as Hanukkah—and in fact I have the actual container. I know the exact words Moses intoned to open the Red Sea. They were omitted from the Bible, of course. I have studied the reasons for the great earthquake that demolished Safed in the nineteenth century, and that had less to do with the will of God than with the actions of a certain Rabbi whose name it is not yet time to reveal, though I can mention that he is still alive. An article I wrote about my quest for the remains of the Golems of Prague was published in the daily papers. My book on the lost Ark was soon to be published—you'd be amazed if you knew how close Spielberg and Lucas came to the real answer—and how far.

There are several self-styled colleagues of mine, though they are hardly worth mentioning: Aharon Reueli is a crook, with his so-called "discovery" of the "actual" Shimon Bar-Yohai grave; Yehonatan Atzil is a buffoon, researching, if such a word can seriously be applied to him, the clearly non-existent sect of Bethlehem; and of course Meir Sassoon, author of the unjustly famous *The Secret History of the Endor Witch*, who is clearly insane. Therefore I am, without doubt, the only Israeli historian of the supernatural worthy of serious consideration.

Imagine, then, my feelings when the greatest supernatural event of the last three thousand years hit Tel Aviv, and I was out of town.

*

Early in the morning that day, I took the train to Haifa. I went there to buy some books for my research, in one of the second-hand bookstores in the Hadar area. I also had to visit Aunt Nehama, my mother's sister. I don't like Aunt Nehama much, I must admit, but Mother insisted. I was there, drinking an unwanted cup of tea and trying to avoid a rather unappetizing cake, when the radio started going crazy.

Unfortunately, at that moment I was in no position to describe what exactly happened in Tel Aviv that day, as I was not there. Fortunately, though, I'd survived, and could now begin my research. Even more fortunate: it was quite safe to assume that Reueli, Atzil and Sassoon were all dead, and there would be no interference.

As we sat there and listened, Aunt Nehama became more and more nervous, worrying for Mother's safety. In the end I had to shut her up, so that I'd be able to concentrate. After some time the radio started repeating itself, as contact with Tel Aviv was lost. This happens every time there's a bombing or a disaster of some sort: the radio and television people have only a very small amount of information, and they repeat it endlessly, like a badly scratched CD. Having had enough of that, I untied Aunt Nehama, set her nicely on the couch and went out to find transportation back to Tel Aviv.

This proved to be a little more difficult than I thought it would be.

*

The first weeks after the event were chaotic. Riots, demonstrations, shootings, people running amok. It took some time for everything to settle down again, and even this relative quietness had many undercurrents. I spent all this time at Aunt Nehama's apartment, only rarely going out to persuade the neighbours upstairs to let me use their shaky Internet connection for research. Only when the mobs were swept off the street, first by the police and then by the army, did I dare to go out.

But then I found that there was no way to get back to Tel Aviv. The police blocked all the roads leading to it and the army guarded its borders, such as they were, and didn't let anyone in. Aerial transport was out of the question, of course—no one dared fly even a kite in a twenty-kilometre radius around the city. Months went by, and I was becoming desperate.

However, no one considered the train.

All the train lines to and from Tel Aviv were cancelled, of course. It was hard to imagine someone being stupid enough, reckless enough, thoughtless enough to, say, *hijack* a train.

Which is exactly where Yehuda Rainbow came in.

The first time anyone had heard of him, Yehuda was an assistant in some archaeological dig near Tiberias. He became slightly famous when, after a night probably spent getting drunk on alcoholic relic cleaners, he tied up every member of staff, filled the main dig with water from the Kinneret, and went to swim in it. He claimed to have been influenced by an alien artefact he found at the dig, but which was never seen by anyone else. The book he wrote about this, after the police released him, sold quite well, I'm sorry to report. What a phony.

You can bet all you want that he wasn't born with that family name, either.

Some of my so-called colleagues weren't as sceptical as myself, regarding this. Yehonatan Atzil, in particular, published several articles about the significance of what he called "The Rainbow Connection," in which he claimed that all this was proof of a government conspiracy to withhold information about UFOs. Which just goes to show.

In recent years Yehuda Rainbow tried several more stunts of this sort, but nobody paid him much attention anymore. Which is probably why I found, in one of the numerous Internet forums dedicated to the occult, a message written in a very familiar style— an open invitation, to those ready to face the unknown, to find the truth lying behind the mundane, etc., etc., to take a train trip to Tel Aviv. Nobody in the forum seemed to believe it, which was fine by me. I knew Rainbow was just unhinged enough to try this. And I was coming along for the ride.

*

The train, which was registered as going to Herzelia, left Haifa just before midnight, the last train of the day. Yehuda Rainbow was driving the engine, but I couldn't see into it. In fact, I'd never even met him in person. He asked that no one tried to enter the engine, and I couldn't think of any reason not to obey. I wasn't interested in him, after all.

During the ride to Haifa, one morning the year before, there was no room to sit anywhere on the train, but now there were only three people in the car except for me, and it was eerily quiet. The train stopped at every station on the way, but nobody came on board and nobody left. There was no talk, no radio playing, no sound but the distant hum and vibrations of the engine far ahead. When we got to Herzelia, the last stop before Tel Aviv, it was past midnight, and very dark. I tried to look ahead but the windows wouldn't open and all I could see was a sort of dark brown fog. I got up and walked towards the front of the train, thinking that I could find a better position to look out. I got to the door between the cars when one of the other passengers spoke.

"I wouldn't do that if I were you," he said.

I turned around, quite slowly, and stared at him. A thin man, wearing a shabby overcoat, which was ridiculous in this weather, and a broad-brimmed hat, which was ludicrous, period.

"Excuse me?" I said.

"We're going into uncharted territories," the man said, a little pompously. "There's a high chance that the train will stop abruptly, or get off the tracks, or do something improbable altogether."

Like rise in the air, I thought. I'd seen the last footage from Tel Aviv before the cameras died. I suppressed a shudder. "That may be so," I said with more bravery than I felt. "So what?"

"So whatever's going to happen, the nearer to the front you are the stronger it's going to be."

That did sound reasonable.

"That does sound reasonable," I said, and—being a reasonable person, after all—I turned and walked back towards my seat.

There was a whining noise, coming from far ahead, a tremendous screech, and then a crash—there was a two-second pause, in which I tried to turn around—then everything flew backwards like a film in reverse as I flew through the door and into the next car, and through that car's open door to the next, and probably the next, which was tilted up, or maybe it was the next one that was tilted, but after passing through the final door I flew high in the air, as if shot by a catapult, and in a split second I was going down, and then there was darkness.

*

I woke up lying on my back in a huge puddle, perhaps a crater filled with water. It probably saved my life. My back and neck hurt terribly, but I was alive and was able to—after several failed attempts—walk. I got up and looked around me. I was at the bottom of a makeshift hill, and above me I saw the Tel Aviv University train station. The train was in the station. This expression now had a new meaning, as the station's reception bay, which is basically a huge piece of concrete parallel to the tracks, was now positioned over them, and the train was stuck in it in quite a literal sense. The engine, which looked rather shorter than I remembered it being, was on fire, and so were the remains of several of the front cars, which were mostly stacked above it at various angles.

I stared at the scene in silence for several moments, then shrugged. *Well,* I thought, *at least that's the last we'll hear about The Rainbow Connection.*

The rear cars were relatively undamaged, except for being one on top of the other, some of them creating the slope, down which I probably flew. I started to climb up, but about midway there was an unexpected explosion and I was buried in dirt. It took me forever to get out of that, and by the time I got to the train nothing was burning anymore.

I managed to enter the car in which I spent most of the trip from Haifa, which now felt as if it had happened a month ago. The door was broken, the windows were broken, but the seats looked as if nothing had happened, except for two dead people sitting on them. One, I saw immediately, had a broken neck, and the other looked extremely pale, as if all his blood had drained away, though I could see no blood on the seat. I didn't bother to check elsewhere.

There was no sign of the man in the brimmed hat.

I got off the train on the other side, the right side, and started to walk. I was in Tel Aviv now, and there was plenty of work to do.

INTERLUDE

The old man watched something amazing, and he sucked on his teeth, which weren't sitting right in his mouth, somehow. He had seen the train arrive, and for a moment time was rolled backwards, and he remembered that day, when he was waiting at the station, and the announcement came over the PA system that the train would arrive in fifteen minutes. He waited, and didn't even notice the strange noises and the spreading darkness, he just waited for Tali to come on the train from Haifa, come to visit her old father in Tel Aviv, and in his mind he made a mental list of things to do together—she loved going to the market, and to eat falafel in that one stand they'd gone to ever since she was a little kid—but he was also anxious, because he wanted her to meet Mrs. Pepper, the next-door neighbour who had recently become more than just a good neighbour. After all they were both widowed now, but he worried how Tali would take it, and so he waited.

But the train never arrived. And there were no more announcements on the PA system, and no more trains, and he remembered the things that appeared, out of nowhere, like winds that weren't winds, that tore and broke and ripped apart, but somehow he lived. But he couldn't know—was Tali all right? Did she stop outside Tel Aviv? Was she safe? Or did her train come into the city and was . . .

So now he searched for her (there was no more Mrs. Pepper), wandering the streets like a ghost, his special Welcoming-Tali-Home clothes dusty and torn and bloodied now, but he kept them on, walking the city, eating from the rubbish other living people left, looting when he could, but it was hard to loot: every gang had a part of the city and didn't tolerate freeloaders. He respected that, respected order, so mostly he ate things he found in the street, and if not he went without. It was all right. He was old and didn't need much food. And for a moment there he thought he had seen something amazing, a train coming into the station, but then he shook his head, trying to clear it. There were no more trains. "When you get here we'll go eat the best falafel in town," he said to Tali, and she smiled. "And then I'll buy you ice cream on the promenade and we can watch the people on the beach, you remember how much you liked that?"

Tali never answered but she smiled and that was enough for him. He shuffled forward and found a pool of not-too-dirty water that had collected in a hole in the road. He bent down on his knees, painfully, and licked the water until he wasn't thirsty any more, and then he went, looking for her in the maze of quiet streets.

SAM: ONE

It started early the previous morning, in Jerusalem, when I woke up from not enough sleep with the phone ringing and my sister's nephew shouting, "Sammy, it's for you!"

I hate when people call me Sammy. It smacks of one of those old cheesy movies with Ze'ev Revach, like *Snooker Party*. But I have to put up with the kid. As well as my sister. And her husband. And their two *other* kids. All crammed into my shoe-box apartment because of—well, you know.

So I took the phone from the kid and I said, "Hello," and it was Y., my boss. And Y. said, "Sam, we need you to come in."

So I said, "Sure," and he told me where to go. Our old headquarters was in Tel Aviv, of course, but afterwards whatever was left of the Service had to move into temporary accommodation near the Knesset building. There was talk of Y. becoming the new Head, but in the event it was K. who got the job, which just goes to show, it's all politics, even national security. I got dressed, and shaved, and had to kick my sister's no-good husband out of the shower before he finished all the hot water. When I stepped out of the apartment the streets were as full as always. You'd think with everything that'd happened there would be less people around, not more, but of course everyone who got out in time, or was outside of the city when it happened, all those people suddenly without homes and shops and offices and jobs—they all came to Jerusalem. So there were a lot of beggars out that morning, and people sleeping rough outside the shops, but they knew not to hassle me by now.

I was a bit surprised, to be honest, because Y. didn't tell me to come to the Service building. He told me to go to the Prime Minister's office. I wondered what could be so important. Maybe they needed me back in London, or Paris. I wouldn't have minded that. Things were a bit rough in the country, as you can imagine. And I always saw myself more as an overseas operative. Well, it figures, doesn't it? I mean, the Service isn't supposed to operate within the country's borders. Which, if I'd only thought about it then, should have given me a warning.

I didn't have to push my way through security. Y. himself was waiting for me outside and he whisked me straight in through a side entrance. "What's going on?" I asked him. He just shook his head and said, "Follow me."

I followed him through the corridors and over to an unmarked door and Y. pushed it open and we went in. Behind the desk sat the Prime Minister.

"Please," the Prime Minister said. "Sit down."

"Sir?" I said. The Prime Minister looked tired. Before him on the table was an open file. I saw my name on it.

"Prime Minister," Y. said, "this is Sam. You remember the Sheikh Al-Nazim incident in Amsterdam—"

Cyanide capsule. Simple and effective.

The Prime Minister nodded. "—and the case of the Hezbollah financiers group in Kuala Lumpur—"

An explosive device hidden inside a laptop computer. Elegant.

"—and that potentially very embarrassing situation with M.?"

"I remember that," the Prime Minister said.

So did I. M. was one of ours. A honey-trap specialist. Until she decided to quit and sell her story to the British tabloids. That one was delicate. It took all of my powers of persuasion to get her to change her mind.

I still get a Rosh Hashana card from her once a year. She lives in Cannes now, and she's married, but . . . some things you never forget.

"One of my best men," Y. said, and I smiled a sort of modest smile, and the Prime Minister said, "We want you to go into Tel Aviv."

I said, "What?" and the smile kind of melted away from my face.

"Tel Aviv," Y. said. "It has been decided that an experienced agent must be deployed on a penetration and surveillance mission into the—"

"But Tel Aviv is within borders," I said, interrupting him.

"That," the Prime Minister said, "is open to interpretation."

I said, "What?" again. The Prime Minister reached into a drawer and returned with two sheets of paper. "These are satellite images," he said, "from before we lost contact. Take a look. This one's from earlier on—"

He pushed the nearer one towards me. I scanned it. A large, sprawling urban area, bordered by sea. A turbulence of some sort on the water, like a gathering storm.

"—and this one from the moment just before we lost contact. Go ahead, take a look."

It wasn't the same picture. Or rather, it looked like a second picture had been superimposed over the previous one. There was a . . . for one thing, there was a great big mountain rising in the middle of the urban sprawl, like something that had *hatched* out of the ground and pushed everything away as it grew. And beyond it were . . .

I said, "What is that?"

"That's what we're hoping you'll find out," Y. said.

Beyond the mountains, barely discernible but *there*, were other mountains, impossibly tall, and a vast plane, and rivers, and—

If you believed the image, beyond Tel Aviv was a new, alien world.

*

The landscape changed the farther away I got from Jerusalem. I drove the jeep down the old Bab el-Wad road, with the remnants of shelled vehicles lying by the side of the road, still remains from the war for Jerusalem all that time ago. The air turned warmer as the altitude dropped. There was little traffic going in the same direction. These days north and south were almost independent entities, with little movement of people or cargo between them. As I drove down the lonely highway towards Tel Aviv I thought of all the times I'd followed this road before, coming in at Ben

Gurion Airport, as the plane doors open and you step out into the hot Mediterranean air and the smell of Israel hits you. It has that kind of smell . . . hot and a little angry and still beautiful, like a woman who is no longer quite young but still desirable. It is a smell made of the memory of oranges, and diesel fumes, and smoke and traffic and brewed coffee and imported perfume. I used to come in to land from some foreign assignment and take the car and drive into Tel Aviv and to the Service building for a debrief. Now the Service was badly hit and I was being sent not to Paris or Rome or Islamabad but Tel Aviv, at least what was left of it.

The farther I drove into Tel Aviv the stranger the land became. The highway here was deserted. There were no cars, no people. In the back of the jeep I had an Uzi and a GPS and some clever toys the boys from R&D gave me just before I left. On my belt was my Desert Eagle .50. I was wearing Ray-Ban shades. I tried the radio but got only static. It made my head hurt and I switched it off.

I began to *see* the city as I drove. Before, it wasn't quite there. You could look directly in that direction and not see anything, or rather, see the *absence* of something, but it was more than that: it was like your eyes couldn't fasten onto what was there and just kept moving away, not registering. But now as I entered it I encountered no resistance.

Driving along, burned traffic signs and places where the road had been jolted out of place. On my left the foundations of a house, filled with water, and dark shapes darting in the depths. I pressed on the accelerator. Tel Aviv's cityscape was lower. The few tall buildings remaining were broken, deformed things. I saw something huge fly high in the sky, swoop once and disappear. As I followed its path I realized the ground had risen towards the centre, and then it was as if I had passed an invisible boundary and—

I saw the mountain.

It rose in the middle of the city like an enormous, impossible island. I could not see the summit. I had the sense of something immense and alien, thought I saw snow-covered peaks in the haze, though that could have been just my imagination, the mind supplying details in an incomplete picture. It was then, while not paying attention to the road, that the wheels all failed at once and the jeep skidded and I lost control of the steering wheel. The jeep swerved and I felt myself rising in the air with it as it overturned, the impact jarring my body, once, twice, and on the third time it stopped. I was afraid it would explode. I unhooked the safety belt and half-fell half-slithered out of the seat onto the hot asphalt, dragging myself away from the jeep. My whole body was in pain.

That was when the attackers found me.

INTERLUDE

There is no more government. There is no more Prime Minister, no more Chief Rabbi, no more *rabanut* to marry you or a *chevra kadisha* to bury you, no more army reserves to call you to duty, no more taxes, no more voting, no more by-laws, no more in-laws. There is no more television. There are no more newspapers. In the ruined coffee shops the tables are empty and filmed with dust and worse. There is no more money, not as it was, not shekels, and there are no more banks. There are no more trains, no more buses, no more shared taxis. There is no longer a Jerusalem, a Haifa, there are no longer weekend holidays to Turkey, no more shopping in London, no more trips to New York. They do not exist for you. There are no more post-army-service backpacking trips to India and Thailand. No more hiking to remote Laotian villages. No more getting stoned in Phnom Penn or Bangkok. There are no more girls to chat up and woo because the girls that remain carry knives and trust no one; no more old ladies to help crossing the road with the shopping, because the old ladies will shoot you if you come too close. There are no more barbershops, no more florists, no more wedding-dress stores. There are no more afternoon walks by the Yarkon river because you are likely to get shot, raped, or captured for the copper-wire mines if you walk there. There are no more letters to arrive, and all the post boxes are quiet and empty. There are no more phones, no familiar voices on the other end, only silence.

There are no more takeaways, no more late-night ice creams, no more hot showers, no more safe drinking water, no more relaxation. There is vigilance and fear and caution and memories of what had gone before, which are best suppressed. The nights are very dark. There is no more Minister of Agriculture, Minister of Education, Minister of Security, Minister of Justice, Minister of Foreign Affairs, Minister of Internal Affairs, Minister of Energy, Minister of Tourism—none of these things exist, and you are the government and the courts and the rabbinic authority, justice and security are yours alone to make.

There is no more before, and there is no more where.

There is only now, only here.

There is only you.

MORDECHAI: TWO

The first place I needed to get to, on arriving in Tel Aviv, was my warehouse, containing my collection of rare artefacts—I had planned to make a museum out of it, though naturally this admirable goal now had to be postponed. It was conveniently located in the basement right under my mother's apartment at the north end of Weizmann Street. It was quite a long way to go by foot from the University train station, especially as everything became more and more ruined and distorted the farther I went. In the beginning, there was only the occasional collapsed building and the remains of some overturned cars, and the major difficulty was the darkness, as none of the streetlights were working. I saw unsteady light coming from behind some buildings, but didn't think it'd be smart to investigate, or even to use the flashlight I had brought.

I couldn't help noticing there was absolutely no one in the streets, nor was there any other sign of life. The noise the train made must have been heard at least five kilometres away, but nobody came to investigate. All was quiet.

It stayed that way until I got to Namir Road and, thinking happily for a moment that about half the distance was already behind me, I first noticed the bonfires.

There were considerably fewer buildings in the western part of Tel Aviv than I remembered, but on top of every one of them there was a fire burning. This was beautiful to see, even amazing, but not as wonderful as the reason I could see all those buildings from my rather low vantage point: this part of the city was now spread upon the low slopes of a mountain.

It vaguely reminded me of a volcano. There has never been an actual volcano in Israel, unless you count pre-history or, God forbid, you happen to get into one of Aharon Reueli's lectures, in which case you are swamped with false evidence that there was one, Mount Sinai, and then wish that a volcano *would* erupt right there and then, to kill the lecturer and, mercifully, yourself, so as to avoid permanent brain damage. I could swear the slopes I was seeing were becoming steeper and steeper the higher they were, but above some point there were no fires anymore, only the feeling of something huge and impossibly tall, a new kind of darkness hovering above numerous specks of light.

As I crossed Namir Road, the main highway coming from Haifa, which was now abandoned and without a single car to be seen, I thought of how this reminded me of Yom Kippur. It's the only day of the year when nobody—well, almost nobody—uses any vehicle other than a bicycle, and everyone, especially the children, walk freely in the streets and on the roads, supposedly asking forgiveness of God and of their friends for sins they'd committed during the previous year, and which they'll be happy to commit again in the new one. It's an eerily quiet day. This was an eerily quiet night.

I hoped that Tel Aviv hadn't become a religious place just because of some perfectly explainable unnatural occurrence.

*

As I continued west I started noticing people. At first only hints, faint noises, monstrous shadows on broken walls, quick flickers of light, something which sounded like a heavy object being thrown into a dumpster. Then, from the roofs above me, talking, laughing, shouting. Then, almost silently, someone small, perhaps a kid, went running past me and disappeared behind a corner. I quickly hid behind a barrel half-eaten by fire, and not a moment too soon, as a gang of five men shot out from somewhere nearby and ran after the fugitive.

I became very careful after that, which slowed me down.

*

When I finally got to my warehouse all was quiet around me. It was already very late at night or, if you like, very early in the morning.

The bonfires on the roofs were still burning, but there were no more voices to accompany them. Everyone probably went to sleep. I needed a good night's sleep myself, but first I had to make sure nothing had happened to my collection.

The first two floors of the building seemed intact. The third just wasn't there. This meant that some of the neighbours, whom I'd known since I'd been born and had grown up with, were probably dead, which was fine with me. It also meant that there was no bonfire on the roof, which was good. At the moment, I didn't need any kind of attention.

I entered mom's apartment, which was on the ground floor, using my own key. I was still living with her when I left Tel Aviv, and I saw no reason to find anywhere else to live, even in the current conditions. I didn't want to wake her up, though—her method of questioning could have been taken straight from the Spanish Inquisition—so I went very quietly, in the dark, down the stairs to the basement's steel-reinforced door, unlocked it, went inside and locked it again behind me.

My hand, by reflex, pressed the light switch. Nothing happened, of course. Either the lines were severed by whatever happened here a year ago, or the city was deliberately taken off the power grid. Instead, I turned on my flashlight. I inhaled deeply. Until then I hadn't realized I was holding my breath.

The secret journal of the Rabbi of Safed. The prayer book which was held by whoever it was who'd built what we call today Noah's Ark. The yet undeciphered writings of the Kinneret Cult. The wooden staff Moses had used to part the Red Sea. And documents, numerous precious documents, copies of items held in museums, articles by archaeologists and historians. Everything was there, in my specially made locked cabinets.

And, in the iron safe, when I opened it—the Hanukkah oil container.

It was all there.

Amid all this, sighing in relief, knowing that everything was going to be all right now, I fell asleep without even noticing.

*

A sound invaded my dream. I wasn't sure what it was, but it was quite insistent. I opened my eyes. All was quiet for a moment. The basement was still very dark, but I sensed daytime. It was hot, and little slivers of light came in through the gaps in the doorframe. I stood up slowly, got my keys, went to the door and started opening it when the sound returned.

It was a man, and he was shouting.

INTERLUDE

It's peaceful on the roofs, one need never come down to the ground. They migrate across the rooftops, a world of dark solar panels no longer working, of abandoned washing never collected from the lines strung under the sun, of barbeque pits and deck chairs no longer inhabited, a wide and open world occupied on one side by the endless sea, on the other by the mountain rising high overhead. They migrate across the rooftops, setting up their tents each night on top of a new building. They hunt the birds that come and settle here, the rats that live inside abandoned buildings, trade self-grown food with the below people, sometimes. Sometimes they catch some of the strange fauna that seems to have come down from the mountain. You learn to love the sensation of peeing from a height, expressing at once your freedom and your contempt for the world below. Titles no longer matter up here. Nor job descriptions. A man could have been an accountant in a previous life: now he is a hunter, a leader of his own small tribe. The babies who are born need never experience street level. They collect rainwater and brew alcohol from fruit when they can be found. There are a lot of things one can find on the abandoned rooftops of Tel Aviv. Sometimes it seems many denizens of that city had never left their apartment blocks, had made entire lives for themselves within, and above. There are storage rooms up here, and some of its hold can be traded. Some roof-people aren't nomadic. Some live on one roof in great green gardens, tiny self-contained Edens they will protect at all cost. The people above are a different people, a new people, and they look after their own.

SAM: TWO

They'd been waiting for me on the Kibbutz Galuyot Interchange. It was my first indication of how bad things had turned out in Tel Aviv, of how far civilization can collapse, and how quickly. They had surrounded me before I could pull out the Desert Eagle. Hands frisked me, stripped me quickly and efficiently of everything I had. Then they turned me over and I got my first look at them.

"Who dis bird hia?"

"What colour gang him wearing? Me no know dem."

They spoke a language of their own, a Tel Aviv argot of the sewers. It was a mix of English from bad Hollywood portrayals of Pacific islanders, and net-speak, and the sort of Hebrew teenagers use. There were about ten of them.

They were all mounted on scooters.

The scooters were painted in slashes of red and white. The men sitting on them had similarly painted their faces. The scooters all had 50cc engines. As I watched, two of them ran to the jeep and began emptying its oil tank. "Dis hia, like, million dolla!" one of them said.

"You, me, everyone rich," the other one agreed. They were very efficient. The oil was transferred into two-litre plastic Coca-Cola bottles, and these in turn were distributed amongst the riders.

I said, "Listen, you're making a mistake. I'm from outside. I'm here to help you."

"Outside! He one crazy mathafucker. Outside. Why he go tellem outside for? Making the boys dey are crazy. I think kill him."

"Kill him!"

"Kill him for sure, or—"

"Yes?"

"Sell him to the Templars?"

"You fucking crazy, man? They'll—"

"Sure, but—"

I said, "Hey," and didn't get any notice. "Hey!"

"What you want, crazy man from outside?"

"Who are you people?" I said. None of them was over twenty-five. Spotty faces. Red and white uniforms. A horrible thought invaded my mind and I said, "You're *delivery* boys?"

"Who you go calling that, boy!" someone kicked me in the ribs. "We is de nambawan gang, Ayalon Highway Chapter, the Street Racers Clan. Why you go talk rubbish like dis, you don't know is dangerous? Close-up you dead, man."

"Look," I said. "Can I stand up?"

"Stand up, sit down, soon you dead same-same."

I stood up. They watched me. I said, "Don't you people speak normal Hebrew?"

One of them, on the far left, young kid with glasses, raised his hand. "Actually," he said, "well, of course we can speak the old language, mothafucker. If only to establish a working relationship with the tradespeople." He smiled at me. "But we choose not to. Do you have a problem with that?"

I said, "No."

"It really is quite easy to pick up, you know," he said, smiling. "There's even an old guy from the university who comes around every once in a while to talk to us. He says he's a linguist, though I think"—and here he switched to their pidgin again— "he like look of boy hia, name of him SpeederManTwo, he want to take boy hia for *ride*, you savvy?"

"Fuck you!" a boy on the right said. I guessed he was SpeederManTwo. I wondered what happened to SpeederManOne. "Why you go make talk-talk like dis? You want fight?"

And then they all began to chant, their palms landing in rhythm on the scooters' handles, and they shouted, "Fight! Fight! Fight! Fight!"

I stared at them, and beyond the city rose, past the ruined highway, and for the first time I truly saw it, the burned-out, broken shell of a city, spreading out for miles in all directions, like a war zone that had been left to stand with no foreign-aid workers coming, a Kosovo, a Beirut, a Kandahar without CNN or Al Jazeera. And beyond the ruined city: the mountain, rising, dominating the skyline, and the sense of slow, immense things stirring, watching—

"Death race! Death race! Death race!" When I turned back to them they seemed to have forgotten all about me. The boy in the glasses and the other one were facing away from me on their scooters. The others surrounded them in a ring. A tall boy in a goatee was holding my Desert Eagle and pointing it at the sky. "One!" he said. "Two!"

"Tree!" they all shouted together, the boy with the goatee pressed the trigger, and the two scooters shot off along the highway. In a moment the others had revved their own miniature bikes and darted off after them, the whole herd making a sound like a cloud of mosquitoes. I heard shots being fired, coming from their direction and, a little later, saw a cloud of smoke rising far ahead. I wondered who won. They made me think of that book they make you read in high school, the kids who get stranded on an island somewhere, I can't remember what it was called. It didn't matter anyway. I think they made a movie out of it. I went back to the ruined jeep. The tires were gone. They must have scattered the road with glass or shrapnel. I picked up my backpack, still at the back of the jeep, and the Uzi, miraculously still there, and stepped off the highway, and into Tel Aviv.

INTERLUDE

Life is better now that the bosses are dead, and the phones too, and life is simpler, and it's good to know all the skills you've worked so hard to gain on the job are coming in handy.

You may ride in a gang, but you only ride for yourself. That is the cardinal rule. You ride for yourself. That's what he loves, the power, the control, as he rides the bike down the empty streets and knows people are watching him from their hiding places, watch him in envy because he has fuel, he has the bike, and in this new improved world he is king. You ride for yourself, but at the same time you ride with a gang, your friends, stronger than friends, your brothers, stronger than that—your pack. You hunt together in the quiet streets and if you see a looter come into your territory you ride him down and play with him, make him run, make him fall, and when you've had enough you tie his feet to a rope and the rope to the bikes and you all ride off together, carrying the garbage outside the border. You share everything with your gang—fuel, food, women—you sleep together, you eat together, you ride together. A lot of it is like back in the army, during basic training, but there are no bosses here, no commanders, everyone is equal, everyone is solitary king of the roads. You speak the language because it is *your* language now, it belongs to you, and each bike-klan has its own, and the ordinaries, the *victims*, the people who used to look down on you and phone for pizza and not tip—they don't speak it, and when you pass by with the engines roaring they skulk and hide and fear you as you pass.

Life is better now, where everyone but you is dead. Life is simpler now, though you will never get to go on that trip to India with Yair, because he's dead now too and there's no way out of the city, and you will never go to the university, because there are no more classes and the university clan, with their unholy engine and their leader who is not quite there, who is not right in the head, who even the bikers fear even if they won't admit it, the university clan doesn't do admissions any more. But life is better now, a man's life, and so you ride: you ride only for yourself.

MORDECHAI: THREE

I froze.

Behind the basement's door I heard a second voice joining the first. Two men were arguing. The sound was muffled, but it was clear that at least one of them was very angry. I tried to put my ear to the door, but that didn't help, I still understood nothing. Then there was a shout, close to the door, too close for comfort, but I still only caught one word. "Something something something, you something something, the Messiah!"

It was followed by what sounded like a punch being thrown, and something crashing on the ground. It could have been one of Mother's old vases, in which case I hoped for whoever had broke it's sake that he died before Mom caught him. He probably felt the same way, since immediately afterwards I heard him going up the stairs and, with a final "Something something—Messiah!" shout, opening the main door and leaving without bothering to close it.

That, if my hearing hadn't deceived me, left me with only one intruder in the apartment. This I could handle.

I walked softly to one of my storage cabinets, opened it, and took out a so-called article by Aharon Reueli. I always collect articles dealing with my field, even if they are written by idiots—a habit of mine which was now going to prove useful beyond its original purpose. Very quietly, I crumpled each page in my hands, until I had several paper balls ready. From another cabinet I dug out the wooden staff which Moses used to part the Red Sea. Perfect. Then I took my travelling bag, which I hadn't even unpacked since the day before, and walked back to the door, slowly, only to realize that it might creak as I opened it. I left the staff and the paper balls there, went to the iron safe, unlocked it and took out the Hanukkah oil container. It still—miraculously—had oil in it. It was useful to the Makkabim, and now it was going to be useful to me. The real miracle was that the door's hinges were exposed on my side, so that I could oil them, which I promptly did. Then I returned the oil container to the safe, and everything was ready for my big escape.

I went back to the door and opened it very slowly. It didn't make a sound. I didn't lock it behind me—if the plan didn't work, I could always run back to the basement and lock myself in, before the invader could do anything. I listened carefully, but heard nothing. It was tempting to think that the apartment was abandoned, but I was sure I had heard only one man leaving. I went up, stood on the stairs with my head just below the floor level, and listened again. Nothing.

I threw one of my paper balls as hard as I could in the direction of the kitchen. I heard it hitting the wall and then fall on the floor. There was a moment of silence, and then—steps. Very quick steps, coming from the living room. I waited for them to get to the kitchen, then raised my head just a bit above the floor level. Indeed there was a man there, bent over to pick up the paper ball. I jumped out, ran towards him and, just as he was turning around towards the noise I made I hit him with the staff. Two-handed, like a baseball player, and smashed it into the back of his head. He went down quietly. My arms went numb. The staff wasn't even scratched.

I took the paper ball and the staff back to the basement, went out again and locked the door behind me. Then I searched the man. He was young—almost a boy, definitely no older than twenty years old—short and mildly muscular, with brown hair and an unsuccessful attempt at a beard. He had a leather jacket, army shoes, metallic-blue sunglasses and no wallet or identification whatsoever. I took his jacket off him, then decided against taking it with me. It stank. But now that I had, I saw on his arm a tattoo: flames, inked in red, and through the fire, eyes. There was something disturbing about the image, though I didn't know what. Beneath it, etched into the man's skin, was something that looked like an over-stylized horseshoe or a magnet, lying on its side.

I took my notebook out of my pocket—I always carry one on me—and copied the symbol. By then the guy was breathing heavily and mumbling. I listened, getting ready to either hit him again or run off.

"Must go back," he said. His eyes were unfocused. I don't think he was even aware of me. "The Voice . . . it says it's time."

"Time for what?" I said, but I don't think he heard me. He was in his own private universe, and he looked scared. "I'm coming!" he said. "Wait . . . wait for me."

"What voice?" I said. I shook him, hard. "What voice?"

"Voice of—" and then something unclear. Then— "Come back . . . all ready now. Must go."

"Go where?" I slapped him.

"The station," he said. He said it as if it were the most obvious thing in the world. And then he opened his eyes, and they were red, a horrible red, so red that they were almost black, and utterly crazy. They were looking right at me.

Then he laughed.

I didn't hit him again. I ran out through the open door, the sound of his laughter following me, and didn't stop until my body gave up and I fell down, winded, on the pavement.

*

I came back to myself sitting on some upturned stones in Jabotinsky Street. It was hot, but the light was dim. There was a redness to everything. And above the eerie quietness I heard weird windy sounds, the kind of noise made by putting a seashell to your ear, only a hundred times louder.

The cityscape around me didn't look any more promising than what I saw the night before. I had to start investigating, and I couldn't get back home, the natural place for doing so—though it may not have been so now, without electricity, Internet access or my mom. I had to do it the old-fashioned way.

Where *was* my mom? And why were there two strange men in our apartment? From my brief look around nothing had been disturbed inside. And I knew my mother enough not to worry about her. It was always *other* people, with my mother, who had to do the worrying.

The Messiah. I shuddered when I thought about the man's insane laugh. What could it mean? Well, some people would think that the Tel Aviv event may have been caused by the arrival of the Messiah, but this line of thought was amateur hour. The Messiah should appear in Jerusalem, not in Tel Aviv, for one thing. And his appearance would look nothing like this. Not according to my sources, at least.

But then . . . perhaps there was someone *claiming* to be the Messiah? Or perhaps . . . perhaps this group, if that's what it was, was *waiting* for the Messiah to arrive? There were more questions than answers, but at least I had a lead.

The station.

There was only one place as far as Tel Aviv was concerned, only one place to fit the bill, one place that would be big enough, impressive enough (if thoroughly cleaned) and comfortable enough to hold an emissary of God and all his crowd.

The white monster, as it was called by almost everyone in the city since it was opened, several years ago.

The new Tel Aviv Central Station.

Only I bet it didn't look that new any more.

INTERLUDE

There is only one synagogue still open that she knows of, and she makes the trip there whenever she can, once a week if the gangs aren't out in force, edging her way through areas that, in her mind's eye, are clearly divided like blocks on a map in different-coloured crayons. If she's lucky they let her pass through, and there are still good parts, still places where people grow their own vegetables, where people share what they have, small communes, urban kibbutzim, and still neighbourhoods where neighbours look out for each other, band together against the gangs, but for her, she has always lived on her own and she does not intend to change, end of the world or not; she trusts in God, despite everything. And so she makes the pilgrimage to the old synagogue where the last remnants of the faithful gather. There are new faiths in the city now. Firemen, horrid godless people, and Templars, and the others, all the others, looking up to the mount as if God resided there, but she knows that is false; God resides in her heart, God is with her as she walks through the ruined streets, and God is there when they gather in the synagogue, though there is no more *ezrat nashim*, no area set aside separately for the women, and never enough men for a *minyan* of ten. But they gather, nevertheless, and they pray, and when she speaks the familiar words she is comforted, and though she is a woman and is forbidden to do so she had nevertheless taken recently to putting on the *tefilin*, which had belonged to her dead husband may-he-rest-in-peace, and she wraps the leather straps over her hand and head every morning and prays: she prays like a man.

She does not believe in a fireman or a new messiah or any of the rumours that regularly sweep through the city like tropical storms. She believes in God, the one God, our God our Lord creator of this earth, amen, and then she begins the long trek back to her apartment, and prays again as she walks that she is not discovered by His creations.

SAM: THREE

Tel Aviv at first glance was deceptively quiet. There were no more pizza-boys on bikes. There were no more people, period. There was a cat, staring at me from the top of a pile of rubble that might have once been a house. The cat was striped orange and its eyes were a strange, deep blue. It stared at me without blinking. I ignored it.

*

They had grabbed me right after I left the Prime Minister's office. There were two of them, big, burly, unsmiling, dressed all in black.

Orthodox.

"Keep moving," the one on the left had said. His heavy rekel coat was open, just a little, and I saw the Uzi hanging down his side. "Chief Rabbi wants to see you."

"Couldn't he just phone?" I said. They ignored me.

A black Mercedes was waiting for us at the curb. They pushed me in the back seat and sat on either side of me. The doors closed. The car glided away.

I sat back, let the air-con wash over me, and sighed. It was turning out to be one of those mornings.

The yeshiva boys took me through the narrow streets to the old quarter of Me'a She'arim, the Hundred Gates community of the ultra-Orthodox. There were posters on the walls advising propriety, and women in black with wigs for hair walking in the streets surrounded by toddlers. We passed a bakery. It smelled good. "Can we stop for a bagel?" I said. They ignored me. "You know, one of the big round ones with sesame seeds and everything?" I said.

The one on my left poked me with the barrel of the Uzi. "Shut up," he said.

I shut up.

We came to a house, though it was more like a stone palace. We drove through wrought-iron gates. Behind the gates was a wide courtyard. More yeshiva boys stood guard outside the wide doors. I was let out of the car. They led me not to the front doors but through a winding path to the back of the house, where there was a small garden, and a wooden shed. They waited outside the shed. Clearly, I was meant to go inside. "Hey, shorty?" I said to the big one on my left.

"Shut up." He didn't have much of a vocabulary. I moved fast. My fingers found his testicles and squeezed. No Uzi can help you there. He dropped to the ground and yelled. I was on the second one before shorty hit the ground, punching him with the palm of my hand, driving the nose bone into his brain, hoping I killed him. They were really pissing me off.

"Enough!" a voice said. I straightened up. There were about ten Uzis pointing at me. Ten yeshiva boys in black, with the wide-brimmed hats that back in the day became the famous cowboy hats of the Wild West. Ten yeshiva boys with guns. Where the hell had they come from?

"Enough," the voice said again, and when I looked towards the shed a man was standing in the open door.

He was of average height, dressed in the same black Orthodox clothes, and there was nothing very remarkable about him—until you met his eyes, and saw the power in them, and then you took a step back.

"Rabbi," I said.

"Sam," he said, and my name on his lips was scarier than anything I'd heard. "Step inside. Please. I merely wish to speak with you." He made a minute gesture with his head and his henchmen hurried to their fallen comrades. The one whose nose I broke was still breathing, though he was going to choke on his own blood pretty quickly unless he got some medical attention. Shorty was out with the pain, whimpering on the ground like a wounded animal. "All you had to do was use the magic word," I said, and smiled, and stepped over Shorty on my way to the shed. The rabbi held the door open for me. I went inside.

*

I didn't know Tel Aviv all that well. I grew up in the industrial suburbs near Haifa, blocks of identical concrete boxes, Soviet-style, where the stench of the Haifa oil refineries filled the air when the wind blew the wrong way. Now Tel Aviv smelled a little like that, and as I walked down the deserted Kibbutz Galuyot road it made me suddenly miss home. My dad moved to Paris a few years after Mom died. We send each other Rosh Hashana cards once a year. I get a call from him every Passover. We talk about the weather. At that moment, with the silence all around me, I wondered if I would ever get out of Tel Aviv again. It felt lonely, and the more I progressed into the city the deeper that feeling got, as if I were the last man on Earth, a Wandering Jew cursed to walk the empty streets forever. At that point the tiger attacked me.

*

"Life," Y. used to tell me when he was still my trainer at the Service, before he was promoted and I became an active agent in the field, "is a series of attacks and counter-attacks. It is true in war, in love, in marriage—" he was breaking up with Noga at the time, though I only found that out much later "—in espionage—" and he made that movement with his head that said, *pay attention* "—in politics and economics and everything else, from your birth to your death. My job is to train you to cope with that. Attack and counter-attack. It's true in music too," he added as an afterthought. Then he took me to the shooting range.

When the tiger attacked I brought the Uzi up just the way I was trained and I squeezed out a round of shots. The sound was terribly loud in the quiet street. I hit the tiger in the head and across the body, and it fell. I approached it cautiously, my heart beating. A fucking *tiger*?

It was dead when I reached it. A pool of blood collected around it. I wondered if I shouldn't skin it. Meat might be hard to come by in the city. But I still had my emergency supplies, and something in me resisted the thought. It looked pathetic. I skirted the body and continued ahead, Uzi held low. It was then I remembered that ahead, at the intersection with Mount Zion avenue, was the Zoological Garden, and I thought—*shit*.

That explained the tiger, though.

I didn't get very far before I heard a noise behind me and, turning, saw the first signs of human life since I left the highway.

A group of children had appeared out of nowhere, scampering across debris, paying me no attention, their eyes focused on the dead tiger. Their hair was long and matted, and none of them seemed to fit inside their clothes properly, the shirts hanging loosely on their bony shoulders. They held knives. When I took a step towards them the nearest one to me, a boy, turned and his eyes met mine. The look in them made me stop. I tried to speak and the boy hissed at me, and at the sound all the other children paused, perfectly still where they were, still crouched like hyenas, and their heads turned to me, their eyes enormous in thin, hungry faces, and they hissed, like one cat warning another from encroaching on their territory. I fell back a step. The children went back to the task at hand. They approached the tiger, in complete silence, and applied their knives to the corpse. In minutes the bloodied pelt was dripping off one of the larger boys' shoulders like a royal cape, and all that remained on the ground was a skeleton with little bits of red meat still stuck to the bones. I watched them throughout all this, repulsed, and strangely afraid. One of the smaller children had brought plastic shopping bags with him, and was distributing them. Each of the children filled the bags with the meat from the tiger. Then, still not looking at me or acknowledging my presence in any way, they scampered back the way they came, and disappeared between the ruins. At that moment, though I had quit three years before, I really wanted a cigarette.

I N T E R L U D E

The children run back to the kindergarten. There are no more teachers, and the sandbox is covered with half-buried human stools. The children speak their own argot: a Pokemon is a corpse with valuables. A Pooh is one that is decomposing badly. A television is anything too large to carry. They don't need television. An ice cream is what's left of a corpse after too much time had passed. Parents are ice creams. A sing-along is any gathering of more than two grown-ups, and must be avoided. A lullaby is a body that isn't dead yet but can be hurried along. Bad Place is what they call the mountain. Firemen are firemen. Firewomen are firemen too. Sick-sick is when you're not feeling too good. Sick-sick is the first stage to half-a-Pooh. They carry the meat as they scuttle and run down the alleyways on the way to the kindergarten. Sometimes grown-ups try to come and see them: groups of scary women who call themselves mothers and want to help them, but they are not mothers, they are cannibals, and if the children find one alone they lullaby it, otherwise they run and hide. Sometimes men come, usually alone, and offer them sweets. Sweets are called choky and are bad for you. Choky-men too. One time a choky-man took Pinky and they never saw him again. After that they mostly hid from the choky-men. They were too dangerous to fight.

They carry the meat and when they get to the kindergarten they sit on the swings and tear into the pieces of bloodied raw tiger, and their bellies are happy and Peretz the Leader, who is the Oldest Kid in the Kindergarten, takes twice as much and is then sick by the petting corner. As night falls they huddle together in the tree house while Simcha Small and Gili Strong keep watch above with catapults. Shiri Sing tells a story and everyone listens. It is always the same story, about the days before time. There were mothers and fathers upon the land in those days. She tells the story of David Smallest, who fought a choky-man called Golgol and killed him with a single stone from his catapult. She sings a song and they all join in and it's like reeds shivering on a riverbank. After a time they fall asleep.

MORDECHAI: FOUR

On the way south I saw more and more of the city. I was now on the low slopes of what I chose to call Mount Dizengoff, which appeared like a wall made of unravelled streets to my right. I saw what remained of the roofs of Ibn Gvirol and Bin Noon streets, as if I was looking at them from high in the air. Higher up, everything was hazy, distorted. My eyes refused to focus on it. And now there were also people.

The first person I encountered was an old woman, sitting on the porch of a ground-floor apartment somewhere in Remez Street, enjoying the light of whatever it was that replaced the sun. I hadn't noticed her at first, but then she shouted, "Hey, boy!", and I stopped and realized that what I thought was a heap of unwashed cloth was, in fact, exactly that but not only that.

"Good morning," I said.

"You new around here, boy? I don't reckon I seen you before."

I didn't know what to say to that, but the woman didn't wait for me to figure out an answer. "You're not one of them Firemen, are you?" she asked, and made a face.

Firemen? Was the Tel Aviv Fire Department still active? Or . . .

"No, ma'am," I said, on reflection. "I'm definitely not one of them."

"I hope for your sake that you're not," she said, with a mean look in her eyes. Whoever those Firemen were, they weren't too popular. I needed to know more.

"So," I said, as nonchalantly as I could, "when was the last time you saw Firemen here?"

"If you don't know that, you're *really* new around here."

"I've been out of touch for a long time," I said. "I was busy. I'm a researcher."

"Oh," she said, and her eyes lit up. "Are you from the university, then? A professor?"

"Well, not exactly, no." No faculty in the Tel Aviv University agreed to accept me, despite all my credentials and documentation. However, in my field I'm the equivalent—at least!—of any professor that you'd care to name, of any faculty whatsoever. "I don't have the official degree, but I'm something very similar."

This, I could see, impressed the woman to no end. "Professor!" she shouted. "A professor!"

"No need to get excited," I said, backing away.

"A professor's attacking me! Help! Help! Save me from the Faculty!"

There was a second in which nothing happened. It was a very long second. I stood there, not understanding what had just happened. The woman looked as if she was going to have a heart attack. Then she opened her mouth to shout again, but just as she was doing so two guys appeared on the porch. They took one look at me and jumped down to the ground. This jolted me out of my frozen stance, and got me running and puffing until Remez Street became Bloch Street, which, mid-way through, became too steep for me to climb.

*

Firemen and Professors. None of it made any sense. Well, actually, I *could* understand why people wouldn't like the professors. That wasn't anything new. The so-called intellectuals with their degrees and their ivory towers, snubbing the unwashed masses, snubbing, more importantly, those of us who had eyes to see what the *establishment* refused to acknowledge. People like myself, who deserved *respect*, deserved to be acknowledged. But no. No wonder the professors were hated. I didn't like them much myself.

But why Firemen?

Was it some sort of gang? Did it have anything to do with the actual fire department? Or with whatever police force was left in Tel Aviv, if any? It didn't seem very likely.

I was walking, thinking of all this, when it occurred to me to look again at the sketch of the tattoo I found on the man at mother's apartment. The symbol underneath the flames—it was neither a horseshoe, nor a magnet. It was the Hebrew letter *Kaf.* I had a pretty strong hunch now that it was meant to be the first letter of the word *kaba'im*: that is to say, Firemen.

I wished for their sake they hadn't upset my mother.

*

By noon I was exhausted. I was hungry and thirsty and awfully tired. The new Central Station was less than three kilometres away, but those were full of ruins and obstacles and people who seemed too aggressive for my taste. I kept myself hidden as much as possible, which slowed me even more. Then I saw the donkey.

It looked perfectly in place, as it came around a corner, walking without hurry right towards me. It was grey and small, and, as far as I could see, utterly at peace with itself and the world. It was also leading a cart. A child was driving it. I watched in silence as it came towards me. Children. There, at least, there was no danger.

The boy shouted, "*Hoisa!*" The cart stopped. It seemed to be filled with old blankets.

The child and I looked at each other. I was thinking of something nice to say, without any mention of Firemen or Professors, and was failing miserably.

"You want something to eat, sir?" said the child.

"Yes," I said.

He turned to the back of the cart, rummaged under the blankets and came back with an orange. He threw it to me. I stuck both my thumbs into the flesh, tore the orange open, and ate it off the peel. I've eaten good food in my life, including an original sample of the manna the Israelites received from God in the desert—which had, I have to admit, tasted a little old. This orange was better. It was better than manna. It made me wonder where it came from. Were people growing oranges in Tel Aviv again?

Or maybe I was just hungry.

"Thanks!" I said. "Can I ask you a question?"

The boy shook his head. "That would be two lira, sir."

"Yes," I said. "In a moment. But first—can you tell me anything about people who call themselves the Firemen?"

The boy shook his head empathically. "Two lira, sir."

"Just answer me first, who are . . ."

"*Two lira. Sir!*"

Lira? That was the currency before the shekel, during and after the British Mandate, a long time before this kid was even born. Was that a joke?

"Here," I said, "take this—" and I pulled out a twenty shekel note from my pocket and gave it to him.

"What the hell's that?" he said.

"It's money, you little—"

He stared at the note critically, making no move to take it from my hand. "Not worth anything," he said.

"Worth a lot more than one orange!" I said.

"You don't have lira? What about a grush?"

"Those coins with a hole in them?" I said, taken aback. Those went out of circulation back in the . . . back a long time ago.

"Yes!" he said. "You have?"

"No."

"What about a quarter-gallon of petrol?"

"What about it?" The kid was starting to seriously annoy me. And I mean—why the lira? Or the grush? Though when I thought about it, it made a kind of sense. There must have been an enormous amount of bank-issued money—of shekels—in Tel Aviv after the event. People must want something rare enough to be valuable. But where would you even get old notes and coins? And then I thought of all the antique shops, and the Tel Aviv Museum, and it didn't seem so far-fetched any more. . .

I wasn't paying much attention to the kid, and I should have been. I should have particularly paid attention to the empty cart, which wasn't empty anymore. The pile of dirty blankets rose and became four men.

They rushed me.

They were big guys, bare-footed, wearing tie-dyed sharwal pants and colourful Hawaiian shirts, paint- or dirt-splattered khafiyas which covered not only the tops of their heads but also their faces. Only their eyes were visible. I didn't like the look in those eyes at all. They looked like murderous hippies who had run out of magic mushrooms.

"Look, I'm sure there's some misunderstanding here," I said, backing away, and then one of them came at me from behind and pain bloomed in the back of my head, and I blacked out.

*

When I woke up I was lying face-down in the cart. It stank of rotten fruit and unwashed bodies. I heard the people talking quietly, above me, but couldn't understand what they were saying.

I didn't want to draw any more attention to myself for the moment, so I stayed as I was and considered my situation. It had obviously been a trap, and I went straight into it. Fine. But what did they want me for?

Suddenly I wasn't sure I wanted to find out.

Try to think of something else. Who were they? I didn't think they were Firemen—no visible insignia, and the man at mother's apartment wasn't dressed like a stoned Bedouin—could they be Professors? Not *entirely* impossible, but hard to believe nonetheless. So they had to be some other group.

How many gangs *were* there in this broken city?

A bare foot landed near my face. Big hands reached for me, turned me roughly around. I blinked in the sunlight.

A face above me said, "Don't worry," which didn't make me feel any better.

"We are," the man said—he had a warm, hearty voice— "the pilgrims, the seekers after divine truth, followers of they who are whole, the holy grail, the multiple manifestations of God, the devouring storm-beings of Altneuland . . ."

For a moment I forgot to be afraid. This was entering into my specialized field. *Altneuland*. That was the name of Theodor Herzl's prophetic novel. The Old New Land. I suppressed a shudder. When the book was translated into Hebrew it was titled differently. It was called Tel Aviv.

". . . the grail which was sent to teach us of the knightly virtues, and the deadly storm that was sent to teach us humility in the face of God . . ."

Oh God, I thought. This can't be good.

"Welcome," finished the voice, "to the Holy Brotherhood of the New Knights Templar." He sighed. "At least until we auction you off."

One year in isolation and Tel Aviv was back to *slavery*? I decided he must be joking. Ha ha. Almost got me.

Don't think about that. Think about something else.

Templars. I knew all there was to know about the Templars, including some facts that were never published concerning the truth behind their "dissolution" and seeming disappearance in the fourteenth century, which, I knew for a fact, had a great deal to do with a certain extraterrestrial artefact. I even know where said artefact was located today, guarded in the Templar's secret headquarters at floor minus-five of the Louvre in Paris. These guys weren't Templars. Not as I knew the term. Which was good, I thought. No worries about being trapped by a world-dominating secret organization then.

No worries at all.

But . . .

Slavery?

Ha ha.

You almost got me.

INTERLUDE

Slavery. There are mines in this new Tel Aviv: there is mining for copper wiring, mining for such things as were buried in the foundations, in the rubble, mining for tins of food in the ruined supermarkets and in the cold dark storage rooms hidden below. It is not a nice place, this new Tel Aviv. There is survival, whatever the cost. There are gangs who seek the weak, the fearful, the ones who are alone, and take them: men and women do this, the gatherers of human souls, and once a month in the old municipality building they come together and there bargain over their pitiful haul, over those few who were not taken by the cold winds of the mountain, and when they are done they set them to work. There are new jobs in this new Tel Aviv, this city of spring and of hope. There are the gatherers, the traders, but worse than them are the overseers who drive the slaves, for they had found freedom in the absence of law, and found power in the dominance of others. There are not many, no. And there are those who oppose them—the Arlozorov Posse, for instance, who fight the traders and kill them when they can, who liberate the unfortunate souls and try to care for them—but how many can you take care of, when you have no guarantee of your next meal yourself? Escaped slaves can sometimes find refuge in the many places of the city—some have become roof-dwellers, some have joined the many tiny kibbutzim that flourish in empty apartment blocks, but for many, capture is almost a respite, an end to running: a final destination from which can emerge only the final, endless peace which had passed them by that last year, yet took their loved ones with it.

SAM: FOUR

I left Kibbutz Galuyot behind me and turned right on Mount Zion avenue. I was watching out for wild animals—and feral children, for that matter, not to mention crazed pidgin-speaking delivery boys and, just possibly, *the* messiah, but all I saw was rubble and destruction, an urban wasteland spreading out and away from me in every direction. I didn't know what Mount Zion Avenue had looked like before the event—as I passed through it all I saw were broken buildings, heaps of rubbish that had once been shops and homes and community centres. I was looking out for danger, but I was thinking wrong—I was looking for *people*.

*

"You are going," the Chief Rabbi had said, "to Tel Aviv."

I nodded. There was no dissembling before the Chief Rabbi. I assumed his own intelligence service was as good as the Prime Minister's. I knew the powers that fought for the balance of Israel. The secular authorities were still standing, but for how long? With the loss of Tel Aviv, Israel had lost the vast majority of its secular citizens. The battle ahead was a battle for dominance, Orthodox versus secular, God versus the godless, and the godless, it seemed, have mostly disappeared in what was clearly a miracle: that is, an act that could not be explained rationally and could not be repeated.

"Do you understand what is at stake?"

I wasn't sure how to answer that. I had the feeling he did not expect an answer. The Chief Rabbi brought out two sheets of paper. Twin images to the ones I had just seen at the PM's office. "What do you think it is?" he said, stabbing with his finger at the second picture. How very Rabbinic, I thought. Always ask the questions. It reminded me of the old joke—how many Germans does it take to change a light bulb?

Shut up! Vee are asking ze questions here!

I looked at the picture. Then I looked at the Chief Rabbi. I said, "I think it looks like a mountain."

"It *is* a mountain," the Chief Rabbi said.

"Do I get a cookie for guessing right?" I said. The rabbi let it pass.

"It is Mount Sinai," he said.

Whoa. And backtrack a little. "I beg your pardon?" I said.

"I accept your apology," he said, and smiled a small, sardonic smile. "Yes, it is Mount Sinai, where God materialized before Moses to give him the Ten Commandments, the basis of all law."

"Mount Sinai," I said carefully, "is, well, in the *Sinai*. That's in Egypt," I added, helpfully. The rabbi gave me a look that suggested I should keep my mouth shut. "God has reappeared to us," the rabbi said. "The time of Moshiach is nigh. The end of days!"

"Wasn't it supposed to happen in Jerusalem first?" I said.

"A technical point," the rabbi said. "Clearly, God felt it was necessary to appear first to those of us who had forgotten the true path. One cannot be only half a Jew. A chance is being given." His look said it was a chance I, personally, should consider taking. I shrugged. "Where is this messiah, then?" I said.

"Aha," the rabbi said. "That is a good question." And again I felt like asking for a cookie. He smiled at me. I did not like the smile. "That," the rabbi said, "is what I want you to answer."

The English have an expression. How the cookie crumbles . . . "You want me to go into Tel Aviv to find you a messiah?"

"Not *a* messiah. *The* messiah. He is there. He must be. If the calculations are correct"—here he tapped the desk, and a pile of computer printouts that lay on top of it—"according to our best kabbalists, diviners and students of the *Torah*, and using the latest gimatria software and bible code decryptors, the messiah would have emerged, unbeknownst, possibly, even to himself, in Tel Aviv, in the area of the event. He would have gone to the mountain, and there—"

"Yes?"

"He would have spoken to God."

"Of course," I said. Of course. There is another old joke—the richest man in the world wants to speak to God, so he goes to the U.S. President. "Can I talk to God?" he says. "Sure," the American President says. "Use that red phone over there. But it's ten million dollars a minute."

Next, the man goes to the Vatican. "Can I talk to God?" he asks the Pope. "Sure," the Pope says. "Use that white phone over there. But it's five million Euros a minute."

Lastly, he goes to Jerusalem, and walks into the Chief Rabbi's office. "Can I talk to God?" he says. The rabbi doesn't look up. "Sure," he says, waving his hand distractedly towards the window. There's a call-box outside, and a queue of people waiting to use it. "It's only a local call."

"What if—" I said, and the rabbi gave me the kind of look that suggested I was beginning to annoy him "—the messiah turns out to be a woman?"

"Don't be ridiculous."

"I'm just saying."

"Look," the rabbi said, leaning across the desk. His eyes locked on mine. "All you have to do is go into Tel Aviv, and find the messiah. Do you understand me?"

"I get you," I said. "I get you."

"Good. Then get the hell out of my sight."

I hadn't noticed the door opening. When I turned around two of the yeshiva boys stood there. The last thing I saw was the fat one on the left smiling. I started to say, "Oh, come o—" and then everything went dark.

*

I was still thinking wrong. I was still looking for people. What I got instead was a—

Something slammed against my back, hard, and I skittered across the road, my body shuddering from the impact with the ground, my palms grazing where I tried to stop the fall. I turned on my back, Uzi drawn—

A great column of air—no, not air—of *nothingness*—no, that's not right either—a turbulence, is the best way I can put it. Not a turbulence in the air, though. A turbulence in reality. The thing was tall, as tall as a building, wider overhead, tapering to a cone where it touched the ground. Though it had no face, no expression, I could somehow tell it was watching me. I nearly pressed the trigger then, but something stopped me. Perhaps the realization that bullets were unlikely to do much to this thing. Make it angry, maybe. I stayed down, on my back, and stared up at the thing.

It was, a part of me had to admit, magnificent. It was like a localized storm, but an aware storm—at least, with a sort of awareness. Not human, not like anything I could comprehend, but when I looked up at it and wondered if it was going to kill me, I felt awe.

The thing moved. The maelstrom passed very close to me. I tried not to breathe. Then, as if dismissing me as irrelevant, the thing swooped majestically down the avenue.

Was this—and others like it—what had caused the devastation in the city?

Yet some people survived. I myself had been left unharmed. Why?

I stood up slowly, my hand holding tight to the Uzi. The thing was moving north along Mount Zion Avenue. I looked north, and up: the mountain rose high above, not Mount Zion, not Mount Sinai either, I didn't think: something else. Something strange and alien and awful, which is to say, it inspired awe. I stared up at the peaks for a long moment. They looked impossibly high.

I decided to continue in the direction I had chosen. Which meant following the maelstrom.

At that moment there was a loud bang, and I dropped to the ground again, hitting my left elbow against the road. The pain flushed hot through me and I cursed. I rolled and brought the Uzi up and then I saw the thing coming towards me, a giant, hulking, snake-like shape, crawling along the road towards me, belching smoke.

I blinked, and stared at it again. I saw multiple eyes on its sides, blinking in the sunlight, and terrible smoke rising from its rear. It swerved and veered haphazardly along the road. It came closer and closer to me, head first, and then it stopped, and I heard the whoosh of opening doors and a loud, ethereal screech that was a car-horn, and a woman's voice said, "Get on! Hurry!"

It was a municipal, double-jointed bus.

I N T E R L U D E

There is an old man living in a public library, and he reads a book a day and when he is done he writes in the margins.

He writes: "Today I ate a frog."

He writes: "Life is a meaningless joy-ride in a stolen car."

He writes: "I am lonely. I want to die."

So far he's worked his way from Aleph to Lamed, and he is halfway through. He knows when he reaches the last book, he will die. He writes: "The city is a furnace, it tempers people into steel."

He writes: "I was once a man. Now I am dead, and do not know it yet."

He writes: "We are all lost."

It is comfortable in the library, and he is safe there. In the piles of books he has dug a hidden entrance, created a small dark space where he sleeps and where he hides when others come in. He always hides. They use the place for a lavatory. Sometimes . . .

He writes: "Were I a writer I would tell the story of this city, and I would tell the truth."

He writes: "The truth tastes bitter and furry. The city lies."

He writes: "Today I ate a rat."

Sometimes he writes phone numbers that no longer work, for people no longer alive. He writes: "I once had a daughter. I once had a boy. I was once a grandfather."

He writes: "I once owned a car. I once owned a house. Once I was with a woman who was not my wife, in Amsterdam."

He writes: "There are no more secrets. There is no one to keep them from."

He writes: "Life is lonely. Death is shared by all."

He writes letters to old friends. He writes letters to the government. He writes letters to the newspapers. He writes: "I ate the body of a badger today. I found it in the Arts Books section." The book in whose margin this is written is covered in stains, like old dried sick. He writes: "I miss her."

He writes: "It hurts to pee."

He writes: "I want to die in Greek Philosophy."

He writes: "Dying in History would be a lie."

He writes: "I am very hungry. There are no more rats."

He coughs a lot, and it splatters the paper. His fingers shake as they turn the pages. He had a name once but he can no longer remember what it was.

MORDECHAI: FIVE

I am not a violent man.

I just have . . . episodes. Sometimes. I've had them since I was a kid. Once, when I was about nine years old, we had a rowing lesson at school. When the lesson ended, the teacher let us jump into the calm water and swim a bit around the boat. When it was time to return, I couldn't climb back on the boat (I was a little heavy at the time). The teacher, who was a somewhat rough man in his forties, shouted, "Jellyfish! There's a jellyfish right under you! Get out of there!" —and I did. I was so scared of jellyfish back then. I jumped on the boat and almost overturned it and everyone laughed at me and I . . .

I don't remember exactly what happened then. Mother had to come to the school and I was excused from gym classes after that, and a couple of the kids never came back from the hospital. My mom took care of everything though. She always does.

But she wasn't here right now, and all I could think about was—*slavery?*—and I was beginning to feel a little strange . . .

"What?" the man beside me said. "Keep still! Hey, help me hold him!"

After that, everything went kind of grey.

When I returned to my gentle, easy-going self, I was standing up on the road, breathing heavily. When I looked around . . .

The cart was overturned, and a plank of wood that previously belonged in the cart's side panel was now in my hand. The man with the hearty voice lay on the ground, unmoving, blood trickling from his head where the wood had connected with his skull. Another man's head was stuck through the wooden floor of the cart, and his body hung limp from his neck. Yet another man lay under one of the cart's wheels, which had broken free. He moaned softly. The fourth man was nowhere to be seen, though I heard running footsteps in the distance. The kid was lying on his side on the ground, giving me a frightened look. I remembered slapping him so hard that he flew in the air and hit the pavement. The donkey, being the only one untouched, stood quietly and looked at all this with a contemplative eye.

I stood up, went to the moaning man and took the cart's wheel off him.

"I've had enough," I said. "Enough mysteries, enough unexplained behavior, enough violence. I am a man of *science!* You will tell me *everything* that you know, right now, or I *will* hurt you."

"You . . ." he moaned, "you won't get anything out of me. You . . ."

I raised the plank. "I will start by cutting off your penis," I said. It felt good to say it. I heard an angry scream from behind and turned around just in time to see the kid charging at me, slapped him again, and sent him reeling towards the overturned cart. "Little shit," I said.

Just then the moaning man grabbed my leg and tried to bring me down. I jumped, stepped on his hand, and then, in a perfect golf movement, hit him between the legs with the plank.

A moment passed in peaceful silence. The man looked at me, then at the plank. I heard the child behind me, cowering under the cart. "The pain should hit about . . . now," I told the man, and then it did.

By the time he finished screaming, the other two men were showing signs of waking up. I dragged them beside the cart and tied them with the blankets.

"Now," I said, "you'll tell me everything. Yes?"

The man I'd sacked sobbed quietly, looking at the ground. There was puke all down his bright Hawaiian shirt.

"Yes?" I said.

"Yes, yes!" the man cried. "I'll tell you everything. Just don't . . . I'll tell you."

"Good," I said. "Let's start with who you people are, and what in God's name is going on in this city?"

"I told you, we are the Knights Templar, we're . . ."

"I don't care what you call yourselves, you idiot. Why did you try to kidnap me?"

"Well, for the war," he said. He said it as if it were obvious. I said,

"What war?"

"The war! The war!"

"You want me to hit you again?"

"We're going to war," he said, talking very fast. "Against the Firemen. Well. Against everyone else, too, probably. Everyone needs bodies, man! Grunts! Foot soldiers! I mean, it's nothing personal! If anyone else saw you walking around they would have grabbed you instead of us! We weren't *really* going to sell you!"

"That's good to know."

"Probably just tie explosives to your body and send you into the—"

I stepped on his fingers and he screamed. When he quieted down I said, "What war?"

"The war against the Firemen. Because of—you know—"

I kicked him in the ribs. "I don't know who the Firemen are," I said. "Why don't you tell me?"

"OK, OK! What are you, from outside?"

"Talk, and make it fast."

"The Firemen," he said, "Believe in the Holy Fireman."

Well, that made sense.

"Really, it's not a joke! Don't kick me again!"

"I will if you lie to me," I said.

"Look, everyone knows this! The Firemen say that there's this . . . thing. This creature who was once a person. But after the . . . the storm-creatures came . . . They say that only the *head* was left, but this head didn't die, somehow it was still alive. The Firemen claim that they have a recording of this head, and it describes everything that happened here, and it contains the story of the Fireman who went to heaven. Don't hit me!"

I hit him anyway.

"I swear this is what they say!" the man said. "Look, why would I make it up?"

Actually, it made perfect sense to me. I was beginning to understand what was happening.

"Why war?" I said.

"Because it's heresy!" the man said. "A holy Fireman? That's crazy!"

Ah.

"Also, everyone else is going."

"I see."

"A Firemen victory could set us back years!" the man said. He was on a roll now. "The assimilation of humankind!" he said. "It is within our grasp! Don't you see? It doesn't matter if we kidnapped you! When this is all over, you, me, everyone is going to join with the creatures on the mount, and we shall be as one, as soon as—"

"Yes?"

"As soon as everyone *believes*," he said. "Or all the non-believers are dead. Whichever comes first."

That, too, made perfect sense. I was beginning to piece it all together now. "And where is this war taking place?" I said.

"The bus station," he said. "Can't you hear it?"

The station. Somehow I wasn't surprised.

As if on cue there was a low, menacing rumble, followed by the sound of an explosion.

"It's beginning," said the man, and there was something I couldn't quite determine in his voice when he continued, "I didn't think it would be so soon."

The second explosion, when it came, lit up the entire sky.

INTERLUDE

I love to go there. It is a quiet, high place, and no one else has found it. I have a telescope, and I carry it on my back, at night, as I walk through shadows, and come to my place, my safe and secret place, the place of seeing. I watch the skies.

These stars are not our stars. Of that I am certain. Sometimes, after sunset or before dawn, I look and sometimes think I see the old stars still there, still hanging in the skies, but they are pale and insubstantial, superimposed over the ones I had recently come to know. Sometimes I see the old constellations but the new ones call to me, the new ones speak and give themselves new names: The Wasp; the Torch; The Infinite Path; The Child; The Burning Man; The Skull.

The Child and the Burning Man are somehow connected. The stars whisper to me, and tell me many secrets. Sometimes at night I hunt the small creatures that still live here, cut open their bodies, spill their tiny intestines into my palm, and read the future in them. Sometimes I train my telescope on the mount, and watch many things, strange and terrifying and graceful. There is always the sense of age beyond measure, of beings both ancient and terrifying, watchers in the dark, indifferent. We are like dust in their eyes, motes of dust tossed this way and that in the air of a sun-lit room. I know what is coming. Sometimes I walk in the streets of this old-new city and I sing, I cry, I call out to my people, warn them of the coming flood. I am Noah, and they shun me as they did him. I know the truth found in a droplet of water, in a grain of rice. I know the truths the ancient stars whisper from their cold heavens. A child will come who is not a child, and a man who is fire, who is more than and less than a man. The world will shake in their passing and be transformed. I know all. Sometimes I eat the small intestines, licking them off my palm, so sweet and salty, and I crunch their little skulls in my teeth. They are so tasty. I am so hungry. I want to be like a star, and never be hungry again.

SAM: FIVE

There were guns going off everywhere and I thought I saw a thirteen-year-old with an RPG on his shoulder *squeeeeezing* the trigger and the wall ahead of me disappeared and I ducked. Shrapnel flew overhead. It was chaos. It was Byronic. It was mad and bad and dangerous to know but I had no choice but to get to know it a whole lot better, or die. Or get to know it a whole lot better and then die. It was a war, and I was in the middle of it. Someone had spray painted a message on the outer walls of the station and I saw it as we approached it and it said, *Welcom to Hell*, and Dganit said, "I hate it when they don't know how to spell."

The bus that picked me up was a very *strange* bus. And Dganit was, if not strange, then at least a very *odd* woman. And the people she was with were even odder.

"Who is this young man?" a querulous voice said when I boarded the bus. The driver was a woman with her white hair tied in a tight bun on her head, and spectacles that perched precariously on her nose. The speaker was an elderly gentleman in a baby-shit brown suit and a large bulbous nose, and glasses. Everyone on the bus were wearing what appeared to be reading glasses. "Why did you let him on the bus?'

The person who let me on the bus was called Dganit. She wore trainers, and grey slacks and a grey sweater, like the coach at a Chinese circus act, you know the one who stands on the side and shouts at the little girl to do it again after she falls from the swing that sits on the rod that extends from a wheel that rotates above a moving bicycle, that sort of thing. Unlike the rest of them she had on dark shades, and across her chest were two bandoliers. She had an Uzi in her hands and what looked suspiciously like a flamethrower on her back. She also wore a hat made of kitchen foil. And two antennas that extended out from her makeshift hat.

"I have been shown," she said, "a great Truth."

I nodded. She turned to the old guy who was complaining and

said, in pacifying tones, "Menachem, we cannot abandon a fellow human being in the middle of everything that is going on right now. He's coming with us."

"What if he's a spy?" Menachem said.

"Then we can kill him later."

Great. The old man looked at me, smiled rather grimly, licked his lips and shuffled off. I wanted to think he had licked his lips out of nervousness, perhaps in fear of me, but I had the awful suspicion it wasn't fear but anticipation that I saw in his eyes.

"My name," said the woman in the crazy hat, "is Dganit. I am the last surviving member of the Israeli UFO Research Society, and the first to make contact—to make first contact—with an intelligent alien life form."

I stared ahead, out of the window. The vortex thing was moving. I looked back at Dganit and swallowed. The only thing I could think of right then that was worse than being killed by one of those things was to be spared by them. Dganit continued, meanwhile. "I have a BA, MA, PhD—"

"Not presented doesn't count!" a voice called from the back of the bus. Dganit turned, Uzi raised. The antennas on her head seemed, for just a second, to actually move.

"Who said that?"

Silence.

"Who. Said. That?"

Silence.

Dganit's head moved, scanning the interior of the bus, where elderly citizens stared out of windows and clutched a variety of weapons. They looked strangely sheepish.

"Gideon, step forward, please," Dganit said. A man in his sixties dressed in tattered army surplus clothes, the shirt too tight over a large belly, rose from his seat and shuffled forward, avoiding Dganit's eyes. "It wasn't me!" he said.

"Get down on your knees."

"Dganit, please—"

"*What* did you call me?"

"Mistress, please!"

"On your knees!"

The man slowly went down on his knees. He was crying quietly. Dganit pulled out a handgun strapped to her left ankle, and put the muzzle to the man's head. "Am I, or am I not Supreme Mistress of the Faculty, Grand Professor and Ultimate Head of Departments?" she said.

"Yes!" The man said.

"Yes *what*?"

"Yes, Mistress!"

"Good. Go back to your seat."

She turned back to me and flashed me a bright smile. "I might have to kill you, of course," she said. "But you look like an intelligent young man. We could use you. Are you currently affiliated?"

"Affiliated?" I said. "Like, to who?"

"To *whom*," she said. "Well, you could be a member of the Firemen, for one—"

"Oh, no, not me," I said.

"He could be a Follower of the Way of Gertrude!" someone called from the back.

"Preposterous," Dganit said. "The heresy has been extinguished with extreme lack of prejudice. Alongside anyone else on Ibn Gvirol Street."

"A Templar—" someone else said.

"One of the scooter clans—"

"But he doesn't have a scooter—"

"Stupid pizza boys—"

"He could be a Child of Two—"

"An Orthodox undercover—?"

"What, you mean without a beard or the black coat—"

"Well, it's *possible*—"

"Indeed. Occam's Razor, my friends. We must always adhere to Occam's Razor. The simplest explanation is always the correct one—"

"Even after the event you still talk of Occam's Razor? And you wonder why you were never promoted?"

"I was never promoted due to jealousy! Envy! How dare you—"

"Shut up!" It was Dganit. They fell quiet. "You, Adamson, and you, Matilda, go to the boiler and change shifts! Make this bus *move*!"

"Boiler?" I said. I did notice the rising smoke, but . . . "You're not running on petrol?"

"Fool," someone shouted. Dganit chuckled, which was a horrible sound. "Conventional fuel hasn't lasted five minutes, as you'd have known had you—hmmm . . ." I did not like that sound.

"Out of town?" she said, speaking quietly. "I've heard rumours, but . . ." she shook her head. "Later," she said, still in the same, soft voice. "We shall talk."

Then— "No," she said, speaking normally again—which, for her, meant screaming in the voice of a sergeant-major— "the few remaining petrol stations are held by our enemies of the various denominations. No, we had to go *green*. We had to go back to *basics*. We had to *re-invent*."

"Steam!" someone shouted at the back. I found that I couldn't distinguish the various cat-calls. They were all elderly, querulous, and slightly absent: they sounded like university lecturers. I said, "Steam?"

"It's a steam engine," Dganit said, and you could smear that pride over bread and call it butter— "a marvel of engineering and ingenuity."

"But, but—but what do you *feed* it with?" I said, perplexed.

She looked at me in surprise. "Well, books," she said.

"Books?"

"Of course. Do you know how many books there are in Tel Aviv? It's a great untapped natural resource!"

"Books," I said.

"We—that is, the Faculty, of which I am Head, hold every branch of Steimatzky's in town! Not to mention the Book Junction, the independents, and the warehouses of the all the major publishers!"

"I . . . see," I said.

"Right now we're powering the engine with as much Amos Oz to get us to the moon and back! And when we run out—"

"You never run out of Amos Oz!" someone shouted at the back.

"We will use A.B. Yehoshua! Meir Shalev! Giants in their field! Mines to be, well—mined!"

"Well said!"

"And if that ever runs out, there's always *The Da Vinci Code*," Dganit said. "Excellent book. Many pages. Burns well. There are tons of copies waiting in the warehouse."

Murmurs of approval from the back seats.

I had a bad feeling about all this. About the bus, its elderly passengers, their clearly deranged leader—but most of all, about their destination. "Where are we going?" I said, trying to sound as polite and harmless as possible.

Dganit looked at me in surprise. "Well, we're going to the War, of course," she said.

I said, "The War?" I was beginning to sound like an echo.

She slapped me on the shoulder in a comradely sort of way. It hurt. "The War!" she said. "The Last and Final War. You know, like in the song? And you'll be glad to know you've just signed up on the side of Right."

I had a sinking, hollow feeling in the pit of my stomach.

The War. The Last, Final War. From the song that said, "I promise you, little child of mine, that this will be the last, the final war of our times." The various members of the faculty began to sing, not very harmoniously. The driver nodded her head and the bus zigzagged this way and that in time with the music.

The Last and Final War.

Right.

THE TEL AVIV DOSSIER

INTERLUDE

A war is coming. We have known it for some time. We are prepared.

A war is coming. A war to end all wars. We are ready. We are armed.

Truth is on our side.

He who has gone shall return again today. This is the time of no-time, the moment of no-moment, the stillness that comes after everything and before nothing. We are the Firemen. We have waited long. We are ready now. Come.

Come to us. Come all you infidels, you non-believers, you who were spared by the one who dwells high up on the sacred mountain.

We have heard the words of truth come from that which should not be alive. Our priests have interrogated the aberration, have divined the signs, have read the map of the world. We who know the *mappa mundi*, we who channel the *spiritus mundi*, we are strong, and we are prepared.

With blood he will come. Sing of us, daughters of Tel Aviv! On the banks of the Yarkon sit ye and weep, and remember what has gone before, for it is gone forever. This is the new age. This is the time of the return. This is the time of our deliverance.

MORDECHAI: SIX

I left the Templar lying where he was, whimpering, the donkey watching him with a bemused expression, and ran, and didn't stop until I saw the station.

The front of the central bus station of Tel Aviv, the largest building of its kind in the Mediterranean, maybe in the world, looked as if a leviathan just broke free out of it. There was a huge hole in the building through which one could clearly see the gnawed support beams of floors 3 and 4. Constant fire was coming out of that hole, and was returned in kind from various points around the perimetre—the windows of surrounding buildings, trenches dug where the road's asphalt was already broken, and, for some reason, people on small scooters. It looked, in short, like a combination of *Die Hard*, *Platoon* and an animated version of *Easy Rider*.

Not my style at all.

I took a long detour around the building, keeping at a safe distance. The whole of the main, long, north-facing front was one constant firestorm. Nothing to do about that. The west side wasn't much better—a tank was trying to break in by brute force, its cannon already twisted like a melted candle. Usually it shouldn't have had any problem doing so, but someone made sure that the whole length of the west wall was covered with boulders and chunks of cement which seemed like the remains of other buildings, creating an uneven slope that the people within the tank were finding difficult to cross. Everything looked so . . . deliberate. As if those people inside had been getting ready for this almost since the day of the event.

The southern side was totally inaccessible. Everything was so twisted and ruined there, on ground level, that the only way in would have been to be shot out of a cannon. I heard some cannons around me, but they, alas, weren't of the right kind.

It took me twenty minutes to get around to the eastern side. There was much rubble there, where the small taxi stand used to be, but there seemed to be some spaces between the stones. What's more—it was relatively quiet.

A slab of concrete from one of the bridges leading to the upper levels of the station fell on the road below, hitting three scooters and raising a cloud of dust. For a moment in the confusion nobody was shooting. I took the opportunity and ran straight into the biggest space I could see, between two sections of what once was the station's eastern wall.

It was cool and quiet inside. I still heard shooting and explosions, but dimly, like a neighbour's television set showing a late-night war film. I relaxed and sat down on the floor for a moment, trying to settle my breath. On one side I saw the dimming daylight. On the other, into the station, there was only blackness.

After a minute of resting I walked inside and, taking special care to see where I was going, immediately bumped my head on a support beam of some sort. I bent down but the space got narrower and narrower, and soon I was reduced to crawling in the dust, cursing this unacceptable war, which was getting in the way of my finding the truth behind all this. The thought of said truth was the only thing keeping me going. That, and the certain knowledge that if not for me, the secrets of the catastrophe would never be revealed.

Not by professional historians of the occult, anyway.

Shudder.

I was making good progress, I thought, and even getting used to the situation, avoiding all sorts of sharp obstacles like broken pipes and metal wires and such stuff as can generally be found inside walls, when suddenly all the background noise—which up until then was audible even inside the tunnel—disappeared. No guns, no explosions, nothing. Nothing but an uneasy silence, accompanied only by groan of the stones around me.

I froze, and that probably saved my life.

There was a low rumble, the ground shook, and something huge crashed just in front of me narrowly missing me. If I was only one metre ahead, I would have been squashed like a bug. I was thinking that to myself, in relief, when the rest of the tunnel fell on me.

That's it, I'm dead, I thought to myself. At least now I'll know for sure what heaven looks like. And, come to think of it, the actual meaning of all those clues in the lost writings of Rabbi Shimon of the Miracle—revealed by myself merely two years ago—whose solution I had hoped to uncover as soon as I was done with the Tel Aviv investigation. Such an interesting experience, death. I wonder why I never thought of it before.

Well, mostly because being dead makes it impossible to get proper recognition while being alive.

But no matter, I thought. No matter. I'm ready. Take me, swift death, quietly and majestically, no more riddles for old Mordechai— only solutions. And what is more dignified than dying in the middle of an investigation?

At which point there came the sound of a tremendous tuba being played by an angry elephant, and the tunnel, the stones, the broken pipes, the wires and myself were shot forward like a brick on ice, and something fell on my head.

*

Someone was shaking me awake. It took my eyes some time to get back to focus, my head was spinning and I was coughing, but finally I managed to see that it was a rather thin man, dressed in an overcoat and a broad-brimmed hat. He looked vaguely familiar, though I couldn't for the life of me remember where from.

"Oh, it's you," he said, looking at me with distaste. "I wondered when you'd get here, you idiot."

INTERLUDE

Hiya, Nicky! It's Shell. I hope you still remember me . . . I don't know if you'll ever get this letter. This is the thirty-first letter I've written.

Recently I've taken to depositing them in post boxes all around the city. Maybe one day the post will work again, and postmen will come in trucks and empty the mail, and send it to you. Like those letters that come back from Everest after thirty years.

I am sad today. I'm sorry. It was a silly thing to write. I hope we see each other soon. Life here is not so bad any more. I am even learning Hebrew—shalom, ma nishma? Beseder, ha'kol beseder . . .

It means, kind of—how's it going? Fine, everything's fine . . . everyone says that. Ha'kol beseder, ha'kol beseder! But ha'kol isn't beseder!

I was so afraid after the . . . when it happened. I think Jason . . . I think he was . . . I never saw him again. For a long time I lived on the beach, we had a small commune going, we shared firewood and food—there are other tourists here, like me, I even hooked up with a Brazilian guy for a while but he disappeared one day, and we thought one of the scooter clans might have got him. You get used to it. There are places in the city you can't go at all. Places where you disappear, forever. You have to watch out for the scooter clans, the feral children, the slavers, the people who are just crazy, even normal people who staked out a territory and would kill you as soon as you stepped over this invisible border.

And now I'm scared. I'm really scared. Nicky, I . . .

I miss . . .

SAM: SIX

There was a huge explosion and a piece of cement the size of a boulder shot out of the building and landed on the asphalt right in front of us.

There were guns going off everywhere. Tracer bullets arced through the sky, many emanating from the upper floors of the giant station. The structure was huge: a white, organic-looking façade glaring down at the army below it. I wasn't sure what was going on: it had something to do with an MP3 player. Partially, at least.

There were two primary competing beliefs, or so Dganit told me. One spoke of a fireman who went up to heaven in a chariot of fire, a modern-day Elijah, and his followers believed that soon he would return. The other spoke of a couple who went up to the mountain, and told that their child would one day return to Tel Aviv; it read like a badly translated version of the Adam and Eve story.

"Where are you in all this?" I'd asked Dganit. She looked at me. Her feelers moved though there was no wind. "We are scholars," she said. "Our position is that the truth must be determined objectively, dispassionately, and logically. Just like we treated the question of unidentified flying objects at the Israeli UFO Research Society."

I thought the logic of that was a bit suspect, but I let it go. "And have you established the truth?" I asked. Dganit nodded and her eyes changed, their colour draining, and a strange, faraway, disturbingly alien look came into her eyes. "I have been shown a great truth," she said.

Aha.

"I have spoken to the minds of the gods," she said. "I have seen deeper into the spectrum of non-human greatness that resides up there, in the heavens of the mountains. I know much that has been hidden."

"Like what?" I said.

She glared at me. Behind us her elderly coterie made gasping sounds. "Nothing your merely mortal mind could comprehend!"

I backed down. She was clutching the Uzi with fingers white with tension. "Fair enough," I said.

"Silence!"

As we approached the station I saw the rising smoke ahead and heard the sounds of warfare. The war was already in progress. I sat next to the old guy, Menachem. He had a window seat now and was levelling a heavy machine-gun through the open window. "Scientists," he told me, "need what we call *empirical proof*. Rumour has it that an object of great importance to the Firemen is secured inside the citadel."

"The citadel?"

"The station. The black tower. Haw haw." It was a strange sound. "You know *Childe Roland*?"

"Was he the British Foreign Office Minister during the Suez Crisis?" I said. Menachem shook his head. "Never mind," he said.

"So what is this object?"

He told me about the MP3 player. And the rumours of a head. And I realized then that, whatever happened, I would have to go deeper yet, into the station itself if I had to, find for myself what was true and what was only story. And then try to report back to Jerusalem . . . I wondered if that was possible. I wondered what was happening in Jerusalem, in the rest of the world. I wondered if I'd ever be able to go back. I didn't have much of a plan, but neither, it seemed, did anyone else.

When we began the final approach to the station I saw the multitudes outside. Everyone who had survived the great event must have been there. I saw flags waving in the air, and recognized none of them. There were jeeps and four-by-fours, two buses, even a wounded tank that somehow still worked and was firing lethargically at the building. I saw scooters and three horses and bicycles with strange firing mechanisms welded to their fronts. There were tents and barricades made of rubbish and bits of houses. The elderly members of the Faculty began to sing again about the last and final war, setting my teeth on edge. Then Dganit said, "Let's go."

On the ground it was worse. There was firing from inside the building, and I saw a woman collapse ahead of me with an arrow through her neck.

An *arrow*?

Dganit said, "We must meet the Council of Associated Factions before launching the attack—" when a rocket coming from the fifth or sixth floor of the station took out one of the four-by-fours and an explosion lit up the sky. Then everything went crazy.

Dganit's feelers shook, and she raised her Uzi in the air and then let out a burst of bullets, and she shouted, "Back on the bus! We're going to *charge!*" and from all around the station people surged forward, a mass wave of insane humanity.

And the war began.

INTERLUDE

Soon it will end. They have come, they are coming still, and the final preparations are under way. Death will call to him, as the bodies pile up he will hear our cry. Two have been called from outside, but more will come, and their fresh blood will sing to the mountain. Let the blood flow: the blood flows, will flow, is flowing. Sing the song of the blood.

The mountain rises above us. We stand on top of a great expanse. The whole of the city is below us. They are drawn to us, like flies to a carcass. They are coming. They have come. they are coming still.

And we are ready for them.

MORDECHAI: SEVEN

"So," said the thin man with the broad-brimmed hat, "Mordechai Abir,
I presume?" He laughed to himself. "In all his glory."

This was rather unfair. I was still trying to get over the blow to
my head, the ground was shaking, the air was filled with smoke and
somewhere too near to us people were shooting at each other.

"Who the hell are you?" I said. Then I realized he was pointing a gun
at me.

"I'd have thought someone with your fine eye for detail, not to
mention your exquisite research skills, wouldn't need to see a person
more than once in order to recognize him."

I examined him more closely. Nothing memorable in the face, except
maybe for the general thinness and the hungry look in his eyes. He was
carrying a nylon backpack over one shoulder. Nothing familiar about
that. But the clothes, the hat . . . where had I . . .

"You're the man from the train," I said. "You're the one who told me
not to stand near the front door of the car."

Something nasty blew up somewhere above us, sending a thin
drizzle of rubble on our heads. The thin man didn't seem to care.

"Indeed," he said. "Not that it made any difference. I should've
known you wouldn't listen."

"But I *have* listened to you!" I said. "Wait a moment, how do you
know me, anyway? No, wait—how did you get out of that train?"

"I jumped out of the window," he said. "Which was just as planned.
Your own survival, however, was a freak accident."

I didn't have any ready answer for that, so I just stared at him. There
was a sound just like a neighbour hammering a nail into the other side
of your apartment's wall, only very loud and horribly fast. Bullets were
hitting the outer side of the building above us.

"If you would have done what you were told, your remains would
still be inside that train," the thin man added. "I should've known
better than to try."

"Who *are* you? How do you know me?"

"Who in the field doesn't know the world-famous historian of the occult, Mordechai Abir?" His words, while being utterly correct, weren't spoken in the tone I'd expect from a serious historian. Which could lead to only one conclusion. A *non*-serious historian.

"I know who you are!" I said, picking a name at random. "You must be . . ."

The thin man smiled. "Aharon Reueli, at your service."

How lucky for me that he didn't let me finish the sentence. I was about to say, "Meir Sassoon."

"I should have known," I said. "The stupid Indiana Jones hat is a dead giveaway."

"I wouldn't mention stupidity if I were you," Aharon said, and I could have sworn that he turned a little red, though it was hard to be sure under the hat. "Not after that pathetic article of yours, on the findings on Mount Sinai. Stupid indeed!"

"I have proof, you ignoramus! I have unquestionable proof, and I can—"

"You have a twig and some antique documents that aren't worth the paper they're written on. I bet you haven't even checked them for watermarks."

Now we could hear shouts, both from inside and outside the huge building we were in.

"Those documents date back from *before* the invention of watermarks, you buffoon!" I said. The man, unsurprisingly for anyone who's ever read any of his articles, was completely out of his depth.

"Which is exactly why you should have checked them," he said, still with that same thin smile. The gun was now trained directly at my head. "Since I estimate your current life expectancy at about, oh, let's say, a minute, I'll just tell you."

I didn't like the sound of that. The gun didn't waver. I kept quiet and he smirked. "If you'd have checked," Reueli said, "you would have found, watermarked in plain sight on all of your precious 'antique' documents for everyone to see . . ."

"What?" I said, with more bravery than I felt. "What would I have found? A photograph of you and your grandmother?"

"No," he said pleasantly. "Just my name and my autograph."

*

Everything stopped.

There was no fight, no shooting, no smoke, no explosions: There was no sound. Aharon's face was frozen. His mocking smile was frozen. The world was frozen. I heard my heart pumping, very slowly and deliberately. Other than that—no movement. The world. His face. His mocking smile.

Slowly, gently, everything turned grey again.

*

"How did you know I would be here?" I said.

"You bastard," he whispered. He was lying on the floor with both his legs broken. Blood streamed out of his nose, and there were teeth on the ground.

"Tell me," I said. "You like to talk, don't you? Tell me or I'll kill you."

"After the train," he said, forcing the words out, "I waited. I saw you getting out of there. Nobody else did. I thought of getting rid of you right there, but instead . . . I went away, I knew where I could start my investigation. And I was right!" he coughed. "By the time I was done I knew this would be the focal point. I got here early on, and waited. I figured that you'd come along sometime. All I had to do was kill you too, and then stay for the final act of my book."

This short speech took its toll, I could see. Aharon's eyes were closed now, and he was taking quick and shallow breaths.

"Your *book*?" I said. "*My* book, you thief!"

He didn't reply.

"How did you find me when I got in, then?" I said. "That was no coincidence, was it?"

162

"Not at all," he breathed. "I used . . . I used the same way to get in myself."
He coughed.

"You *waited* for me," I said. "You wanted to tell me, to my face,
how you ruined my life's work, and then, with me out of the way,
you would have gotten all the credit for researching the Tel Aviv
Apocalypse . . ." and then something he said finally registered and I
said, "All you had to do was kill me *too*?" and I saw the hint of a smile
in his eyes.

"Remember Meir Sassoon?" he said. "The guy who wrote *The
Secret History of Ein-Harod*?"

Of course I did. That idiot. That, as I was being told, dead idiot?

"He stayed here," Aharon said. "He collected all this crazy stuff,
you wouldn't believe it. Recordings, writings, video, digital, it's a
treasure. It's all here . . . I had to kill him. I couldn't let him . . ."

"You would have done it yourself," he said.

His eyes closed.

I nodded. Then I took his backpack, strapped it over my shoulders,
and walked away from the gunfire and explosions, inwards: towards
the centre of the station, into the heart of the awaiting darkness.

PART FOUR:
WAR

I. In the beginning was the Fire.

II. And when the fire raged upon the deeps He came.

III. The First Fireman.

IV. And He battled the emissaries of God, Creatures of Wind, and bested them.

V. But the world lay in ruins, a desert, and he traversed it to the Mount.

VI. And the Mount rose up to the heavens, and God lived on its summit, and God's creatures dwelled in the lower slopes.

VII. And God spoke to the Fireman.

VIII. And God sent Him a Sign, and the Sign, too, spoke to the Fireman.

IX. And the Sign was a woman's Head. And the Head loved Him. And He spoke to the Head, and when He was done He released it, to go amongst His people on this earth, and speak of His return.

X. And seeing that all was as it should be, He rose to the heavens in a Chariot of Flame.

SHE: ONE

In the beginning was the womb, and somehow she knew what it was: it was comfortable and warm and as she grew she became aware of her mother and her mother's thoughts, and learned much about the world. There were refugees in the world from a place called Darfur, and there were women who sold their bodies in the place of transport called the Old Bus Station. And there were monsters dwelling upon the earth in those days. Creatures of wind who came from the sea and ravaged the city which was called the Place of Spring, Tel Aviv, where white buildings rose up to the skies before the other world came and dwelt in its midst.

Being born was like travelling through a tunnel of light and emerging into sensation. Fingers on her tender body, and wind and air and the smells of campfire smoke and the taste of her mother's milk and the warmth of her father's chest as he held her close, and so much to see, mountains and springs and snows and trees and birds.

"She is not meant to grow so quickly," her father had said, and she knew that he was worried for her. They moved often, camping in caves and in the open savannahs, and she soon learned how to hunt and skin and cook, for the smaller creatures of the mountains had never seen a human being and were not afraid.

"The Garden of Eden," her father often declared, and her mother snorted but said nothing. And her father told her stories: of Adam and Eve, of a Tree of Knowledge and a snake, and of a flaming sword that turned every way. And her mother told her of the suffering of Women, and of Patriarchal Subjugation, and the Importance of Rebelling Against Orthodox Hierarchy, and her father sang to her, children's songs about donkeys and goats and birds, and told her the legends of Solomon, who was a wise king, and how he met Asmodeus, the king of the demons, and how he fell in love with the Queen of Sheba, and how she tested his wisdom, and the story of the flowers she presented to him, and challenged him to find the real one amongst all the artificial ones, and how the king followed the path of a lone bee as it traversed the field of flowers, and came to land on the one that was true.

They moved a lot, and when it rained, sought shelter in the nooks and crannies of the great mountains, and watched the passage of the great wind beings, thousands of them at a time passing across the plains, and her parents were awed, while she felt a yearning inside her, to be with them and soar with them into the air.

Always the mountains rose above them, and the higher they climbed always the peaks were farther away. They traversed great chasms, hiked upon glaciers as ancient as any world, and she knew them all, knew their names and their histories and could summon the small, shy creatures of the snow and the veldt. Time had no meaning there, and her parents watched her grow with love but also with concern, and one day her mother said, "You'll be a woman soon," and sighed, and her father hugged her mother and she saw the love between them, and felt a momentary emotion she did not at first recognize: jealousy.

Though they disagreed on most things, on the subject of love her mother and father were in agreement. They told her stories of the way they once were: her father pale and studious and unhappy, sitting in a place called a yeshiva, which literally meant a Place of Sitting, and her mother always running, always on the move, a thing called a camera in hand, always documenting other people's lives. She could not imagine them so: her father, strong and brown from the sun, a silent hunter, her mother the same, and both content, both in love and loving her too, their daughter, and so they lived and much time passed there, on the eternal mountains, with only the wind and the wind's children and the strange animals of snow and earth for company. And so time passed.

SHE: TWO

One day they had traversed a fold in the mountain and a strange sight was revealed, and she felt uneasy and did not know why. Her parents had gone very still. Her mother came to her father and he held her in his arms and neither looked away, though they looked as though they wanted to do nothing else. In silence they stared at the valley below, and it was like nothing she had ever seen.

Burnt mountains rose up from that valley. Blackened stumps like grasping fingers reaching for the sky. They had no natural shape. Squares, white squares, blackened as if by an immense fire. Her mother cried, silently, and her father said, "Tel Aviv," but still she could not grasp it. The valley below was man-made, her father said, and her mother said, "man- and woman-made," and her father said, "Of course, that's what I meant."

It was made by people. It was the place they often talked about, the Spring, and she was horrified by it. And though it was terribly ugly, there was, strangely, beauty in it too, and she felt herself restless, and didn't know why.

The wind picked up then, a cold clean wind that swooped down from the mountain to the valley below, and when it returned it was warm and carried with it strange scents she did not know, and sounds, and the sounds were harsh and alien and she felt herself shiver, and her father said, "They're shooting at each other!"

And her mother said, "So they are still alive. There were survivors after all," and her parents held each other closer still. And her father said, "But for how long?" and his face was troubled.

Her parents made to turn away from the sight then, but she did not turn with them. For a long moment she stood and stared out at the miniature world spread out below, and she felt many sensations, like hot and cold currents running through her, and a voice seemed to whisper in her head, the way it sometimes did in the isolated places of the world, and she listened to it, though perhaps it was only her inner self that was speaking to her in her own voice.

Her parents turned back to her, and she saw in their faces that they knew her thoughts, and were troubled by them. "Come with us," they said. "Come back to the high places, where the air is cold and clear and the silence speaks only truth. Come back with us to the great open spaces where the children of the wind run and play. Come back with us—"

They fell silent then, for they knew her mind, and knew it could not be changed. And so they approached her and held her close to them, and her mother stroked her hair and her father kissed her brow, and she saw them both cry and felt wonder.

And so, at last, she bid them farewell; and carrying no burden, but that of love, she travelled down into the world of women and men.

THE WAR

1.

At first there's nothing to be seen, and almost everything to be heard. Small arms fire, an occasional explosion, bullets hitting concrete, glass, tin and flesh, each with its own distinct sound, and the shouts of the attackers, the defenders—though there's no knowing who's who—and mostly of the wounded and the dying on both sides. Those are the obvious sounds. But also: the ominous creaking of heated metal; the hiss of water running out of punctured pipes, along with a hint of a louder gushing—someone on the western side has found a hydrant and is using it to repel anyone who's trying to access level 6, or at least that particular section of level 6; the groans of the support beams, trying to redistribute the weight of the shifting parts of the building; and, somewhere on level 1, which is actually a sub-level—frightened whispers and a child crying.

More than smoke, there's dust. It hovers in the air, making everything grey and stuffy, and gradually it muffles even the strongest sounds. It is as if the dust has waited there all along, since the station was first erected, to be liberated from the shackles of a closed and ordered space, to get up and around, to be free, and now there's no getting back from this murky revolution. So for now, everyone inside goes by sound.

Somewhere on the eastern side of level 4, which is in fact the ground floor, a historian of the occult—or so he likes to think of himself—is trying to find his way out of the maze created by a bazooka hit that drove a part of the outer wall inside, right through a considerable number of gift shops. He is entirely focused on his destination, and therefore fails to notice the fact that the floor is wet, and that this wetness stinks. A sewer pipe right below him was cut in a recent explosion, and dirty water has been draining into the rubble for some time now. Soon, when the water level rises a little, it will register with him. Meanwhile he knows only that to get the answers he needs, he must find a way up, to the top levels.

At about this time, in another part of level 4, a steam-powered bus is driving right through the front entrance of the station—which was recently and violently enhanced, and is now big enough to let it through—ignoring the heavy cross-fire. It runs through a series of stalls, and before long it is covered with brightly coloured T-shirts, summer dresses, umbrellas and smoking teddy bears. As it finally stops, hitting a concrete wall, it farts a huge mushroom of steam, which momentarily and unintentionally distracts the snipers on levels 5 and 6, thus saving the passengers—who are now jumping hurriedly out of its windows—from being picked off like the main course in a sitting-duck banquet. The passengers—all of them but one—gather around a thin woman in her forties wearing a tinfoil hat and sunglasses. There is a hurried discussion among them, and then they decisively turn towards one of the escalators leading to level 5. The one passenger who doesn't join them, an agent of a government service that does not, officially, exist now crawls out and gapes at his surroundings. He's been through a lot of strange things in his life, but this is definitely on a different scale. A burst of gunfire misses him by sheer luck, and he runs, finding temporary shelter in a nearby men's room. There he stops to think. He knows now that to get the answers he needs he must find a way up, to the top levels.

Somewhere on level 1, despite the best efforts to make him stop, a small child is crying. He too knows, by instinct, that the answers to many questions lie up on the top levels. However, he isn't looking for them. He just wants all of this to stop. He wants silence. He wants the grown-ups around him to stop crying.

A tremendous explosion comes from outside. A mine just blew up one of the bridges leading from the bus platform on level 7, and then the whole building seems to jump in the air as one hundred tonnes of concrete falling from the 4th floor hit the street. For a moment, the crying child gets his wish—everything stops. There's an eerie silence, disrupted only by the sounds of the tortured building. The silence holds for almost ten seconds. Then everything starts again.

Except for the child. He's quiet. He stares up at the ceiling. Something is happening there. He doesn't know what it is, but it looks wonderful.

2.

This part of the station was converted, who knows how many years before, into a mall. It consists of several floors running along the outer walls of the building, while in the middle there's nothing but air. This way, from each floor one can see all the others. Thus, when the dust settles a bit, at last, it reveals a view that would have delighted M. C. Escher.

There are stairways and escalators lying on their sides, leading nowhere. In many places, support beams previously hidden inside walls or shops, sometimes covered in various items for sale, are now naked and exposed, and in most cases also alarmingly twisted. Level 6 now sports a surprisingly large waterfall, running uninterrupted right into a former gift shop on the ground floor, which momentarily looks like an aquarium, all sorts of debris swimming inside, until its glass walls—miraculously surviving the fighting so far—can't take the strain anymore and blow out.

Everywhere there are piles of broken concrete and metal and junk. Some of them are still smouldering. Some seem fused together. Almost each and every one of them has at least one human being trying to climb it. Like ants, or termites. Or like some sort of liquid, an undercurrent, digging its way up, always up, towards the top levels.

*

Mordechai Abir knows a thing or two about undercurrents slowly digging their way up into the foundations of seemingly stable structures, which then seem to suddenly collapse for no obvious reason, creating chaos. He could give, as an example, the eruption of the First World War, which wasn't really the result of the murder of the Archduke Franz whatshisname, nor of secret agreements between the great powers of Europe, but had more to do with the activities of the Rosicrucians and the Freemasons, and most of all the unnamed cabalistic sect whose members, men and women, held places of power in both secret societies. He could cite many other examples, which he honestly believes are true, of such subterranean rivers undermining the ground above them. It's just that, until now, this never happened to him personally.

This particular ebb, current or river consisting mostly of sewage has, by now, with the addition of the water from the level 6 waterfall, rightfully earned the esteemed title of Flood. Mordechai, who was caught off guard, first ran, but soon found out that it's almost impossible to do so when the water reaches one's knees. Now he's flopping around, instinctively trying to keep dry the backpack of precious documents he has stolen from a rival occultist, despite his former loud-spoken denial of their authenticity. He keeps stumbling upon all sorts of trash that should've been easy to avoid were it not currently underwater—pots and plants, bags, trolleys, suitcases, toys and abandoned weaponry. He's trying to get to the nearest heap of debris, not too far ahead, but progress is slow, very slow. It seems to him that each sloppy step in the muddy waters takes forever. Meanwhile he can see other people climbing the heap, people getting there ahead of him, crawling up. It's frustrating. It's maddening. Eventually, it saves his life.

There's a high whistle from far above, crazily ricocheting between the huge walls of the station. Then there's a groan, as if something big is being moved despite its best efforts to stay inert. The historian looks up just in time to see the front half of a double-joined bus being pushed from the top level, falling right at him.

He's frozen, crouching there in the stinking water, during the very long half a second of the bus's fall. He thinks of nothing. His mind is blank. Then it occurs to him that, if not famous last words, he should at least have anonymous last thoughts. Then the bus crashes on top of the heap of debris, about twenty metres away, and squashes it. Mordechai Abir is thrown off his feet and collapses face down in the water. When he surfaces, the bus stands half-sunk in the water, its broken headlights facing Mordechai in a menacing stare. There's no junk heap. There are no people.

There's no way up.

*

Sam meanwhile has found a way up. He's now climbing one of the elevator cables, and prays to God and to any other deity that may be listening that the elevator he can see four stories above him is safely secured in its place. There's a scary moment when something quite heavy crashes to the ground, somewhere outside the elevator shaft, and the cables begin swaying crazily. He clings to his spot, forcing himself not to move, not daring to look up. He whispers curses to himself. He curses the Prime Minister, the Chief Rabbi, the Service. He curses himself. Stupid, stupid, stupid. Getting stuck in this hellhole, and for what? Nothing. If he doesn't die falling from the cable or having an elevator come down on his head, he'll probably get shot when he gets up.

The movement slows down, then ceases. The agent relaxes his grip, just a little. Nothing happens. He fights a sudden urge to let go, leave it all, fall all the way down, end it quickly this way. He also fights the urge to pee.

Instead he starts climbing up again.

*

The child looks up. There's a fine web on the ceiling, thin lines emanating from a point right over his head. Bits of plaster are falling here and there, but none of the grown-ups around him seem to notice. Near the centre, a part of the ceiling seems to be pulsating.

Maybe the lines of the web don't really glow in the dark, maybe its lines aren't silvery beams of light—maybe it looks that way to the child only. Maybe the web isn't there at all.

As the child watches, it grows.

3.

The historian has managed to find high ground on top of a former T-shirt stall. He sits there, half covered in dirty wet cloth, and considers the backpack he took from his rival. His enemy. There's a good chance he won't make it out of here, and he must at least have a glance at these documents. He opens the backpack and looks inside. It's filled with nylon envelopes, watertight. In each of them are sheets of paper covered in print. It looks like it was done on a manual typewriter. The letters are small, and there's literally no space between the lines. He reads:

THE FIRST CHILD'S STORY (RANI, APOCRYPHAL)

Shula, our neighbour from the second floor, just flew like Superman out of her window. I saw that because I was looking at the things outside, and she passed right in front of me. I want to fly too, but Mom will shout at me if I try . . .

He reads:

NAAMA—PODCAST II (DIGITAL AUDIO)

My voice sounds weird. I can feel nothing below my neck, but there must be something there, otherwise I wouldn't be able to talk, having no lungs. Otherwise, come to think of it, I'd be dead. Or am I dead already? Does it matter? Maybe it's a hallucination—they put something in my food. In my drink, some gas in the air conditioning, some . . .

He reads:

THE FIREMAN'S GOSPEL, PART VI (ELI—APOCRYPHAL?)

It was love at first sight. The moment the disembodied head flew into my cabin, it fell in love with me. Don't ask me how. Or why . . .

He reads on. The documents are strange. Illogical. What do they have to do with anything? And if they do—how were these testimonies taken? Some of them are by people who are obviously dead. Others . . . or maybe it's just a sick joke of the historian's rival, not a mere forgery like his previous trick, but something more complicated, a scheme so ludicrous that it might look true? It's insane, it can't be, it should all be thrown away—but he keeps reading.

Meanwhile, another group of attackers enters, this time trying their luck with a heavy machine gun, which they station on top of the ruined bus smashed in the middle of the floor. They manage to shoot several rounds of ammunition before someone up above has enough and a liquid of some sort comes pouring down on their heads. Their screams are terrible. Terrible enough to jerk the historian out of his stupor.

He knows that staying in one place isn't a good idea. Definitely not this particular place. He needs to get up, and he needs to make it clear that he isn't on one of the warring sides. That he's not dangerous. That he comes in peace.

He looks around him, but sees nothing that would be of any help. No way of communicating, and no one to communicate with. Then he glances at his immediate surroundings, and has an idea. He rummages through the pile of shirts, all wet and covered in plaster and ill-smelling. It occurs to him that, at this stage, the same description could well be applied to himself. He's dripping water, his hair plastered over his head like a wet mop, and . . . well, he just wishes that his sense of smell would go away. He keeps taking shirts out of the pile, throwing them away. Then he finds one that fits his needs. He takes it. Like all the rest, it stinks of sewage.

He wrings some water out of the shirt. He reexamines it. It's disgusting, but it'll have to do. His mother, he suddenly thinks, would have beaten him with a candlestick for even touching such a foul thing. Maybe even for being in the general vicinity of it. He almost smiles at the thought. Almost.

He needs this shirt. It's not really white, but for his purposes it's white enough.

He spreads the shirt as wide as he can, and holds it over his head. Then he steps, waving it, to the fallen half-a-bus, surrendering himself to whoever may be watching from above.

*

Sam is now right under the metal floor of the elevator, parked at level 6. Before attempting anything else, he's trying to listen. Are there steps above? Is there someone inside the elevator? There's no logical reason for anyone to be there—he would bet his ludicrous monthly pay cheque on the fact that there's no supply of electricity anywhere in or around Tel Aviv—but then, nothing in his experiences of the last two days has been dictated by logic. So he crouches over the lower elevator brakes, hugging the thick cable, and listens.

There's less gunfire now. Ammunition must be running low on both sides. Instead there's a steady series of thuds. Somewhere out there things are falling. He guesses that the dwellers of the upper levels are down to throwing projectiles at their attackers. He concentrates again on listening but can hear no steps above, nothing to hint at an ambush. He'll have to take a chance.

He finds what looks like a small service door in the elevator's floor. He gives it a push. For the briefest of moments there's the hiss of a sound: the murmur of oil in a roasting tin, the sound of flesh sticking to burning metal.

Sam screams.

*

Traditionally, when a Jewish boy turns thirteen, a Bar Mitzvah is held for him in the synagogue. After he finishes reading his *haftarah* from the *Torah*, the newly Bar Mitzvah'ed child is bombarded with a considerable amount of candy, thrown at him by the women and children who watch the ceremony from the place allocated to them, usually on the second floor. This is a sign of festivity.

Right now, the mall looks like a bloated version of a gigantic Bar Mitzvah party that went berserk. All sorts of objects fall down— and are thrown down—from the high levels: stones, scrap metal, bus tires. One imaginative soul on level 7 is pouring burning oil over the edge, just missing a group of attackers on the ground level. The boiling drops of oil-spray in the air, however, can still burn, and the attackers hastily retreat to relative safety behind a broken part of the ceiling, which fell down a little earlier. Occasionally bigger things are thrown down. Nothing as big as the half-a-bus thrown several minutes before, but still they make an impressive impact: motorbikes, refrigerators, toilet bowls, a Coca-Cola dispensing machine.

It is quite a miracle that none of this has hit the historian so far. Mordechai Abir walks slowly, waving the off-white shirt over his head. He feels like a ghost, wandering through this scene of carnage. No one seems to notice him, he thinks. Then something hits him from above.

Mordechai screams and jumps. Then, seeing that nothing has actually happened to him, he looks around. There is a piece of rope hanging from above. He looks up and sees someone waving at him from the upper level, beckoning for him to climb up. He goes to the rope, pulls at it. It seems steady. He climbs.

There is shouting on the floor around him. People are running towards him, some of them waving weapons. The historian was never good at climbing, or at any sport, and now he's regretting this bitterly. The rope seems to become more and more slippery. Or is it just that he's sweating? Wild parties of attackers, looters, whatever they may be, now surround the rope on three sides. Some of them throw stones at the historian, who has so far reached only half-way to the upper level. Then, from above, comes a warning shout. The historian almost loses his grip as the rope starts, as of its own accord, to rise, lifting him with it.

When he reaches the level above, strong hands grab him. He's gasping, there's blood on his wounded hands, and he's almost crying with relief. He collapses on the floor. "Thank you," he says. "Thank you!"

"Looks like Mommy plucked herself a little chicken," someone says, and chuckles, and as Mordechai turns, with quite a lot less relief now, to see who's talking, a blow to the head knocks him out.

*

Sam is in hell. Or, at least, his right hand is in hell. The heat comes from the metal handle of the trapdoor. It is a searing heat. The smell of his burning skin makes him ill. He kicks at the door but it won't budge and he screams, in pain and anger.

When the door opens at last it takes him by surprise. It opens downwards. He is captured in large hands. His own hand is now covered in first-degree burns. The pain and the stench of his hand make him gag.

"Watch it!" someone says. Then he is lifted up, easily, and dropped on an enormous shoulder.

It feels a little like when he was a kid, and his parents played Bag-of-Potatoes with him. He is carried without effort. There is something feminine about the figure carrying him.

She says, "Mommy is going to be pleased."

*

The child is still looking up. The fine web has spread on the ceiling as far as he can see. Now the lines seem to be thicker, and in some places there's no mortar anymore, just exposed concrete. The grown-ups don't seem to notice any of this. Some of them are crying, others are shouting at each other. It's dark and dusty, but the child sees everything quite clearly. He's strangely calm. Everything seems to him, now, like a dream.

A stone falls from above, then another one. Suddenly it's not dark at all. A shining ray of light comes from above, from the ceiling's centre. Like a theatre spotlight, it illuminates the child. The grown-ups, instinctively, back away.

"Mommy?" the child says.

Then the ceiling collapses, burying the lot of them.

SHE: THREE

The children retreat to the kindergarten carrying Peretz the Leader, the Oldest Kid in the Kindergarten, with them as they retreat. There is a sing-along of adults gathering, more than they had ever seen, and they are frightened, and Peretz is sick-sick, sick-sick bad, on his way to half-a-Pooh in a hurry-up. They make a fire and let Peretz shit in the sandbox and his shit is all runny and it smells real bad and Danny Small-Small begins to cry. The sky above is lit with loud sounds and flashing lights and over in the Bad Place that rises above them there is a sense of being watched—the Big Choky-Man, they call him, the Old Bad Man of the Mountain, and they're all afraid.

Simcha Small and Gili Strong keep watch like they always do but suddenly there is a birdcall and it's Gilad Two-Finger, the lookout running back, and he says, "Www-www-www—"

"One—" Gili Strong says. Two-Finger nods. "One www-www . . . www . . ."

"Woman?"

Two-Finger nods. Gili says, "A mother?"

"Dddd . . . dddd . . ."

"Don't know?"

Two-Finger nods.

There had not been mother incursions recently. The women who periodically try to take the children had mostly given up, or died, become ice creams. They'd been repelled by catapult and cunning. "There are no mothers!" Peretz says and his little hands are shaking. "N . . . no more mothers. Lullaby her."

Kill.

They'd found a Pokemon that morning, lying by the side of the road, already beginning to smell, on its way to becoming a Pooh. They got a pistol off it, and Gili Strong takes it now and she says—

"Lead us to her."

But there is no need. Because just then Two-Finger lifts his hand, where only the two middle fingers remain, and he points up, and they see the woman, and behind her the mountain seems to shiver, and the sun comes out and the woman seems to be glowing and Shiri Sing says, "Ohhh . . ."

The woman looks at them and they see her face and it's strange, it makes them feel . . . they don't know how it makes them feel, but they all share it, that sense, like going back, like remembering something good that had happened, once, long ago, in a place you thought you'd forgotten. And the woman says, "You're children."

There is something awful in the way she says it. Two-Fingers bursts out crying, and Peretz sits down in the sandbox and shivers and doesn't say anything. But Gili Strong, who is the strongest, lifts up the gun they took from the Pokemon and she points it at the woman—and the woman smiles. She has a nice smile. It is a horrible smile. Gili Strong feels her hands shaking. The smile reminds her of a face she used to know, a face that was always nice to her, that held her close and sang to her and rocked her to sleep, and she says, "No!" and she presses the trigger.

There is a loud explosion, and the recoil throws Gili Strong on her back and the gun falls from her hands, and some of the smallers start crying.

When Gili Strong looks up again the woman is still there, and she says, "You don't have to be afraid any more. Everything is going to be all right." And she bends down and pulls Two-Finger close to her and he doesn't resist, and she hugs him. And then Shiri Song goes to her and the woman hugs her too, and then all the kids rise, and they approach the woman, slowly, shyly, and when they come to her she holds them all and she rocks them and she sings to them, and she says, "Don't be afraid of the Big Choky-Man. Don't be afraid of the sing-along of grown-ups. Don't be afraid of the sick-sick and the Pooh and the Pokemon. Everything is going to be all right now, children." And the woman is smiling, and the woman is crying, and where she cries the tears fall down on the children's faces and on their hands, and when Peretz, last, comes to her, the tears touch his face and the colour returns to his cheeks and soon he's smiling and he's no longer sick, and the woman says, "Hush now, all of you, children, children!"

After a while, the children sit up, and the sun is shining, and they had been sleeping, even the watchers. The woman is gone, but somehow she is still there, too. Gili sees the swings and without thinking she goes and sits in one, and rocks herself, and Peretz comes and gives her a push, and she laughs, and Peretz goes, "Whoosh!" and Gilad finds new crayons and white paper so clean and white it's blinding and he draws happy faces; and the smallers play in the sandbox, which is clean and full of cool sand. And they build mountains.

THE WAR

4.

Now there's a lot to be seen, but the sound is muffled, filtered, on the verge of the unreal. This, on the very top floor of the station, is the bay from which people used to start their journeys across Israel—to Haifa and Naharia in the north, to Eilat and Be'er Sheva in the south, to Jerusalem and the Dead Sea in the east. Now no one is going anywhere, and the only vehicles to be seen are the cannibalized remains of intercity buses. The bus-bridge going down from the bay to the ground was blown up earlier, though in the confusion no one can tell who was responsible. The bay looks like a giant wrecked porch, with a nice panoramic view to the south where a wall of dirty, blood-coloured clouds separates Tel Aviv from the rest of the world. Right on the edge, from which one could freely fall the height of four or five floors to the ground, someone positioned weird contraptions made of red leather and cardboard and metal and plastic junk. They look like dust motes the size of small cars. Whatever those things are, they seem to be on the verge of falling apart.

The wall separating the bay from the rest of the station is relatively intact. Only one hole has been blown in it, quite some time ago. From this hole now emerges a column of people—five, ten, thirty. They all wear red. Bright red T-shirts, shiny red nylon raincoats, red pants, red dresses, and even, in one case, a red bikini. Between them they carry seven big bamboo cages. Inside the cages are seven men, all in various states of unconsciousness, none of whom is wearing any colour worth mentioning.

The leader of the group, a small figure covered, despite the heat and terrible humidity, in a thick dark red robe, hood included, raises a red-gloved hand. The procession stops, and the cages are lowered down to rest on the floor. By what is, perhaps, a strange coincidence, each cage is located right beside one of the weird leathery contraptions lying on the edge of the bay. The carriers straighten up, salute, then stamp their legs together on the floor.

This noise, finally, reaches into one of the cages and wakes up Mordechai Abir.

"In the beginning was the fire," says a voice. "And when the fire raged upon the deeps He came. The first Fireman."

*

Sam too has awoken. His first emotion is anger. First, his hand. Then his captor, a moving mountain shaped like a woman, carrying him like a baby, paying no attention to his protestations or his cries of pain. Then, when he tried to fight his way free—a slap from her hand, just that and nothing else, but so hard that he flew against the wall, banged his head against it and lost consciousness.

Now he has regained consciousness. His second emotion is fear.

He is trapped inside a bamboo cage. Somewhere nearby, someone is making a speech.

The voice is sharp and precisely articulated. Every syllable is in place, every consonant loud and clear, every comma an absence, every period a void. It is an old voice, but he can't tell the speaker's gender.

His third emotion runs close to despair.

*

"And He battled the emissaries of God, Creatures of Wind, and bested them," says the leader. "But the world lay in ruins, a desert, and he traversed it to the Mount."

The red-gloved hand points upwards. This, Mordechai Abir thinks inside his bamboo cage, is really quite fascinating!

It's as if he's found a lost tribe, previously unknown to modern man. This is exactly what he was looking for when he came to Tel Aviv! This, as opposed to all those documents he's been chasing all these years, this is the real, authentic thing. Fascinating!

185

And yet . . . as he huddles inside his cage, he can't but wonder where it would lead. The anthropology of cannibals is a lot less . . . fascinating . . . when it is you yourself who is inside the pot.

*

"And seeing that all was as it should be, He rose to the heavens in a Chariot of Flame!" intones the leader's voice. "And as He rose, so shall we rise, so shall we rise so that He may return!"

To which the whole congregation answers, "So shall we rise!"

"Firemen—to your positions!" shouts the leader.

Strong hands grab the cages, open them, drag the prisoners out. The agent tries to fight, but his whole body is cramped. He can't even stand, and thus has to be held. He catches the mocking glance of the woman who caught him, towering over the leader like a storm front. Then his hands are shackled and he is dragged and tied to something, some contraption that smells like rotten leather and paint. He knows then that he was right. It's going to be bad. He just doesn't know how bad.

*

Seven men are tied to seven contraptions. All around them, red-clad people operate, fixing, staging, pulling and tying things. Each assembly of leather and plastic and junk slowly gains a more defined shape. The operators scurry around, tightening ropes, setting levers. Then it is all done and the operators return to a safer distance from the bay's end, on which are now positioned seven red, part-leather, part-human bats.

"To the fire ye shall soar," says the leader, "and in your trail the Fireman shall come!"

A prisoner shouts, and immediately receives a wooden club to the head. The rest of the prisoners, learning fast, settle for quiet moans.

186

The leader raises both hands towards the congregation. "Bring—the Lover! Bring the bearer of the prophecy! Bring the receiver of fate, the recorder of the miracle, the speaker of the truth!"

A small procession now comes out of the station, seven women wearing black robes. The last of them carries a big silvery box in both hands. She stops in front of the leader, gently puts the box on the ground, and opens the cover.

No-one is talking. Even the prisoners understand, however dimly, that something of importance is happening. Now there's a sound, the sound of wind, the sound of a storm. The air is charged.

There's movement inside the box. Something rises. Something round and brown. It's furry. No, it's hairy. It keeps rising. It's a ball covered with hair. No.

Rising, higher and higher, like an awful jack-in-the-box, is a severed human head.

SHE: FOUR

Shell wandered through the streets and didn't know where she was, or where she had been, and there was a great pain in her head that wouldn't go away. Occasionally she whimpered. There was blood on her head, and on her breasts, and her clothes were torn, and she ached. She once had a friend but she could no longer remember her name. She once lived in a house where hot water ran, and had showers, and there was a white magic box that kept food inside it. She once had parents who loved her. There was a lot of noise and she couldn't think. The very earth trembled. There were explosions, and screams. Where was she? She didn't know this place. It was a maze she had to walk. Her feet were raw and bleeding. She hugged herself and tears streamed down her face. She didn't even know she was doing it. She no longer knew how to cry.

Then she heard a voice, and the voice said, "Shell" and, since it was her name, she stopped and turned. "Shell," the voice said. "My poor, poor Shell."

There was a woman standing there. Shell couldn't quite see her face. She seemed wreathed in light, but maybe it was just the way the sun came down at an angle. Shell, in a small voice, said, "I want my mommy."

"Oh, Shell," the woman said, and she came to her, and held her, and Shell felt herself letting go against the woman's body, and she cried, and the woman stroked her hair and said, "There, there," and patted her on the back until she made Shell burp and then laugh, and then cry again. "Everything will be all right, Shell," the woman said. "I promise. And your friend's name is Nicky."

"Nicky," Shell said, and a look of wonder came into her eyes. The woman said, "Why don't you sit down here, in the shade, and write her a letter, Shell? You'll be safe here."

"I think I'll write her a letter," Shell said. "Nicky. How many letters did I—?"

The woman seemed to smile through the shimmer of light, and shake her head. "No, Shell," she said. "You've only written the one long, very long letter. But you should be able to finish it soon."

"That would be . . . nice," Shell said. She sat down where the woman suggested. It was comfortable there. Somehow there was paper and a pen, as if they'd been waiting for her. She sighed. It felt good sitting there, writing to her friend.

"Dear Nicky—" she started. When she next looked up the woman was gone.

THE WAR

5.

In the bay on the top floor of the station there's a human head hovering above a crowd of several dozen oddly dressed people. The head, which seems to have once belonged to a brown-haired woman, now sits upon a whirlwind emerging from its severed neck. It looks like a monstrous lollipop. Its mouth is closed. It says nothing.

Most of the people below—those who aren't tied to anything at the moment—are chanting and slowly dancing in their places, without moving their feet off the ground. They raise their hands towards the floating head, either praying to it or encouraging it to perform some atrocity. Without haste, they begin to remove their clothes.

The floor is now covered with red. Red robes, shirts, coats, pants, underpants. Among the piles of clothes there are also various weapons—hunting rifles, pistols, old army M16s, some bows and arrows. The only person still fully dressed is the leader of the group. Still hooded as well. The chanting and dancing continue. The head is still silent.

The leader, raising both hands, shouts something incoherent. The singing stops. The dancing stops. Everyone is watching the leader. Even the floating head. Then the leader says, quietly, "Rise."

Nobody moves. Several floors below there is the sound of a firefight and an internal wall collapses, but here the noise is merely an echo. Nobody moves.

"Rise, O Fireman!" says the leader, and the first line of believers takes one step forward, towards the edge of the bay, towards the seven captives held in their fragile contraptions.

"Rise, O Fireman!" shouts the leader, and suddenly Mordechai knows what these things are, and he screams.

They are kites.

"Rise, O Fireman!"

The kites are grasped by strong hands, lifted into the air.

"No!" Mordechai shouts. "Wait!" but his voice is drowned, and the other captives are shouting now too. As Mordechai is lifted higher, right above the edge of the bay, he sees the ground several floors below.

The leader gives one final shout, loud and clear above everything else, and takes the hood off her head. It is a woman, and she is terribly familiar to Mordechai. "Rise now!"

A gust of wind grabs the kites, lifts them higher, higher still. As he is being thrown over the edge, off the roof, the historian cries, "Mother!"

*

At first Sam fails to understand why it is that he is not dead yet. He does not expect these homemade kites, this combination of twigs and leather and old wire, to hold him in the air. He expects the ground to come rushing at him, and is rather surprised when it doesn't.

A warm wind blasts from the north, bringing with it the smells of cooked meat and gunpowder, and something else, too. There is the smell of weird, improbable animals and strange trees and wet soil. These smells cannot be coming from Tel Aviv. Sam realizes he is smelling the mountain.

The wind grabs the sacrificial kite, throwing it up, above the bay, above the watching believers, above their leader who now, without her hood, is revealed as a small, elderly lady. The wind carries the kite above the hovering head. If the head is saying something, Sam cannot hear it. His ears are filled with wind.

He looks around, seeing some of the other captives flying around, above and below him, each moving in a different direction but covering the same small area. Flying in circles, he thinks, as the ground and the station turn gently below him.

Then there's an ominous creaking sound and the kite starts coming apart.

*

Seven broken swans hover impossibly in the air, dangerously close to each other. The wind seems to be pushing them together, higher and higher, but one sees the distorted shape of the wings, as various poles and sticks and beams break or fall down. The small human forms at the bottom of each kite now visibly squirm, like earthworms exposed to the light. Higher and higher they go, seven Icaruses ready to fall.

The head looks up. It opens its mouth. And a turbulence appears in the clouds barring the view to the south, an ochre-red whirlwind of dust.

Something is moving there.

Something is coming.

6.

Everybody—the believers, their leader, the squirming captives hung in the air under their rapidly disintegrating sacrificial kites, even the hovering head—all of them look towards the wall of clouds. It seems to be sucked into itself, then it expands, stretching forward towards the city. A red bubble appears in it, slightly above the roofs of the remaining buildings, and with it a sound, like a faraway chainsaw in slow motion. Both bubble and noise grow, become more violent. Then there's a crescendo, and something bursts out of the cloud wall.

It's a helicopter.

It's flying straight at the station.

*

There is a moment in which everything seems to hang in the air, on the verge of falling. This, of course, has been true for the seven captives for some time now.

The helicopter is a Bell Boeing V-22. *This is strange*, Sam thinks as he is strapped to the breaking kite. To the best of his knowledge, no such aircraft has ever been purchased by the Israeli Air Force. It's huge. And it is painted a cheery light blue.

As the helicopter reaches the station, hovering above the bay, above the kites, Sam feels the wind of its rotors. It blows the kites downwards. Then a door opens in the helicopter's rear and something falls out of it. Then another one.

Sam looks up and thinks, *Paratroopers.* The sky is suddenly filled with opening white parachutes, and on every one of them is painted a large, blue Star of David.

As they descend, Sam notices the paratroopers are wearing black. They cradle weapons in their arms.

When they start shooting, Sam recognizes the so-familiar sound of an Uzi.

He almost sighs with relief, then. He knows where the helicopter came from. He knows who these people are.

The Chief Rabbi's army has arrived. Yeshiva boys in parachutes, raining fire from the sky.

*

Mordechai Abir is also on the verge of falling. He hugs his kite, hugs his still-dripping backpack filled with documents, holds on for dear life: He can't focus on his surroundings. All he can think about is his mother. His mother. Impossible. Unbelievable. *Mother can't . . . mother won't . . .*

But deep in his heart he knows that she always could, and maybe that she always did. She was unstoppable. He just never imagined . . .

And he thinks—that's why there were Firemen in her apartment.

His glider is lower now. A great wind comes from above, pushing it down. Tracer bullets also come from above, though it appears he is not their target, at least not yet. There are shouts from below. Many believers are already down, spraying red blood over red clothes and the dirty tiles of the bay. His mother, however, is still standing. He wants to call her. It must be a dreadful mistake, he thinks. She had no idea that he, Mordechai, her *son*, was one of the captives. As far as she was concerned, he reasons, he's still in Haifa, and safe. How could she have known?

But he knows his mother. She knows everything. She always did.

He watches her take something out of her robe. It's a long-barrelled gun, at least a .44. She raises it, takes aim.

She fires seven times.

From above, seven cries. A red rain begins to fall.

*

As the seventh paratrooper dies, something happens. A change of wind, a shift of colour, a new spectrum of sound, as if a huge red piece of cotton was taken out of the world's ear. The head opens its mouth wider. Its eyes glitter.

It roars.

Everything becomes yellow. The station, the clouds, the people, the very air. Everything is hot, on the verge of burning. A wave of heat strikes from above. Flames erupt from the kites, from the clothes on the bay's floor, from the few parachutes still in the air. Heat beats upon heat.

The captives fall, one by one, back onto the bay. By now they are not too high above it, so in the event, only three of them die from the impact, neither of which are Mordechai or Sam.

There is a brightness above the helicopter, a flame, beside which the huge flying war machine looks like a mere toy. Something is happening up there, but the people below cannot discern details. There is a grinding noise, rising and rising. The ground shakes, the whole station serving as the world's biggest speaker set, amplifying the sound, sending an awful wave of bass towards the skies.

The helicopter explodes. Parts fly in all directions. One of its rotors slices an already-dead paratrooper in two.

In the place where the helicopter hovered just a moment before, something else appears.

The head's roar gets even stronger. Its gritty treble rivals the station's bass.

The thing in the middle now acquires a shape. It's red. It's big. It shouldn't be hovering in midair, but it is.

It's a fire truck.

.

SHE: FIVE

There are twenty-seven members of the Rooftop Players Commune and they don't want anything to do with this. With any of it. The bikers are kooky kids, the Professors are idiots, the Firemen nothing but hooligans. The Rooftop Players isolate themselves from all these groups as best as they can. The Rooftop Players believe in peace, and love, and music.

They have their own rooftop in one of the previously industrial buildings of Hamasger Street. They have built a crude wall around it, so that no one can see them. They built a primitive elevator from ropes and a plank of thick wood. They grow their own food, they raise their own children. They have three guitars—two acoustic, one classic—and at all times there's music playing. Songs by the Beatles, imagine all the people, and by Jimmy Hendrix, little wing, oh, little wing, and by Led Zeppelin. When someone gets tired of playing, someone else takes over. For some reason they can't explain they've been playing "She'll Be Coming Down the Mountain" all day today.

Those who don't currently play or take care of the children or sleep are busy making love. There are twelve guys and fifteen girls, and of those, seven are already showing signs of advanced pregnancy. There are neither condoms for the Rooftop Players, nor pills. There's only love, and love is free.

They don't remember how long they've been this way. They don't care. The beards on the guys faces get longer and longer. There are two pairs of scissors on the roof, but they're rarely used. They elevator themselves down only to fetch water or look for more canned foodstuffs, but they try to make those trips as short as possible, get back to the roof, where it's safe. They feel like they could live like this forever.

But today something is different. Since midnight there's no playing on the roof, no more music. A wave of nervousness passes through the Rooftop Players, and they sit quietly, separated, wondering what has happened. They think, each of them, they may have seen something strange and wonderful, a woman wreathed in light, passing down below, but it might just be the mushrooms.

Nevertheless, the image lingers, makes them restless. One of them stands up and goes to the elevator, lowering himself from the roof to search for water and food. Then another one goes. And another one.

After some time there's no one left on the roof. The Rooftop Players walk, each submerged in his or her own thoughts, passing through streets that are no longer empty. Others walk the streets today, emerging from basements and fortified apartment blocks, from petrol stations and bookshops, from hidey-holes and safe houses, women and men, the young and the old, all who still remain. They think not of the war, not of safety or survival. None is aware of the others. Yet they all head in the same direction. All following the path. Her path.

Heading south.

Where the Central Station lies.

THE WAR

7.

In the awful light of the burning helicopter nobody notices the one remaining living paratrooper landing on the roof. He cuts the ropes and his parachute goes free, a huge prayer shawl flying away to the east. He lies on the floor, on his back, breathing heavily, looking up.

There's a fire truck in the sky, and it's coming down.

*

Sam fails to believe what he's seeing. At first he doesn't believe that the Chief Rabbi's paratroopers were taken down so easily. Then he can't accept the helicopter's destruction. And then, then there's the fire truck. It's huge, it's red, and it's surrounded by tongues of fire. It simply can't be. He thinks maybe there are hallucinogens in the air. Maybe he's tripping. Maybe he's dreaming. Maybe he's not even in Tel Aviv, but drugged and locked in a cell by some terrorist organization, and his mind is trying to come to terms with the situation by inventing this elaborate story about a city wiped off the face of Israel. Maybe there was no meeting with the PM, no deal with the Chief Rabbi, no mission, nothing. Maybe he's old, stuck in a home for the terminally ill, passing his days in happy delirium.

But he's not happy. He's not happy, and there's a huge red flame-throwing fire truck in the sky, coming down, coming down, growing larger in the skies above. It isn't possible, yet it must be true.

That's one hell of a report I'll have to write, he thinks.

The fire truck keeps coming down.

*

Mordechai is struck with awe. As he watches the truck, slowly rotating around its vertical axis and spitting flames in all directions, he thinks of an old film he once watched, *Close Encounters of the Third Kind*. He feels as if he's starring in the climactic scene of that film, watching an alien spaceship descending, looking for a way of communication. He remembers how it was done in the film—by music—and for a moment regrets his lack of dedication to the piano lessons his mother forced him to take when he was a child. That thought brings him back to the present, and he starts looking for his mother. She stands near the edge of the bay, training her gun on the descending fire truck. Her hand is steady. She doesn't even blink. He knows better than to try and call her right now. Another film comes, unbidden, into his mind . . .

The Wizard of Oz. Right after Dorothy lands.

The fire truck lands. And Mordechai Abir screams.

Feet sticking out from beneath the great red vehicle . . . for a moment he thinks his mother's feet are going to curl in on themselves and disappear below the engine, but no: they merely shudder, once, and are still.

*

For a moment, everything is still. Then there's a sound, a scream of concrete rising from the very heart of the building. Pressure has been mounting and the building isn't taking it well. The floor hums like an ungrounded electric bass. Then the supporting beams can hold it no more and it falls.

From above, it looks as if the building is being blown up from the inside. As level 7 becomes level 6, then level 5, the surrounding walls fly outwards in a whirlwind of cement and dust. When it stops, half a floor above level 4, there's a crash that could be heard several kilometres away, were there anyone there to hear it.

The reason for this becomes clear to the survivors of the former 7th level as they get up from the floor—which has strangely survived the fall in one piece—and try to dust themselves. They look at the fire truck, which is still standing there, still burning, and then they notice the rest.

Around the Central Bus Station is a crowd of forty thousand people. Everyone left in Tel Aviv.

They're quiet.

They're waiting.

There's a hiss from the fire truck. From within the flames, the form of a man appears. At first he seems like a mere shadow, but then he grows, fills up, solidifies. In a voice as loud as a foghorn, as dry as forest fire, he clears his throat.

There is a moment of silence. There is a moment in which time changes, when future becomes present, when present becomes past. There is a moment in which everything halts, fragments, reshapes itself into words, a narrative of human time.

Every human moment is a beginning, and an ending.

PART FIVE:
THE LAST TESTAMENTS

I have seen much that was previously hidden.

I have known that which cannot be spoken of, but fuck it, let's mention it anyway. I've come to tell you. Everything.

I have felt the cold winds that lash the body into a thousand fragments of pain. I have dwelt in the dark places, and grappled with the ancient ones, and saw into their minds. And I have learned this:

The universe is a cold, dark place. The universe is a cellar, in which humanity are prisoners. The universe has no meaning beyond being. I have seen it. I have passed through fire and was unharmed. I have passed through pain and was unpained. I have seen the world spread out before me like a thing spoiled—a rotten carcass left in the field of battle for the carrion crows.

I have come to tell you all this.

Blessed are the mean, for they shall be triumphant.

Blessed are the cold at heart, for theirs shall be the softest bed.

Blessed are the bullies, for to them is promised the kingdom of heaven, where the cold uncaring spirits of the mountains dwell, the masters of creation by dint of teeth and talons, of power and aggression.

Blessed are the pimps, for they sell love but are not slaves to it. Blessed are the sick, for their path shall soon come to an end. Blessed are the meek, for their bones shall bleach white on the highway of life, rich pickings for the rest of us.

You have waited for me!

And I have come.

Do not rejoice! Do not light a candle under a bushel or on a candlestick. Put it in a petrol station, and watch a multitude of cars blow up. Put it under the feet of men who are not worthy. Tie it to the tails of cats, or foxes, like Samson did.

Think not that I come to destroy the law: for there is no law. I have come to destroy. Yes. If there is anything left to destroy, I shall destroy it.

For I say unto you: do not be righteous pricks.

Drink. Smoke. Fuck. Do unto others what you have always wanted to do. Because up there, there is nothing that cares for you.

You are like ants to the things on the mount. And they, in turn, are gnats to the greater, older ones, those who put out suns and freeze oceans, who hurtle black holes into populated planets. There are many worlds. They all suck.

Verily I say unto thee, thou shalt by no means come out thence, till thou hast come out farting. And if thy right hand offend thee, cut it off, and cast it from thee. And the same with your left eye. Or your testicles.

For you have heard that it hath been said, an eye for an eye, and a tooth for a tooth. But I say unto you, that ye resist not evil, but embrace it. And whosoever shall smite thee on thy right cheek, raise your leg to him, and knee him in the balls, and kill his wife and kids, and eat his dog.

Lay not up for yourselves treasures upon earth, where moth and rust doth corrupt, and where thieves break through and steal. Keep them on your person, and keep a gun, too, and shoot to kill. For where your treasure is, there will your heart be also.

The light of the body is the eye: if therefore thine eye be single, thy whole body shall be full of light. But if thine eye be evil, thy whole body shall be full of darkness. If therefore the light that is in thee be darkness, how great is that darkness!

I have seen the darkness. It is great indeed.

Forget God.

If God was a prisoner he'd be someone's bitch. They'd be building Route Six through his asshole by now. Fuck God. Fuck him up the ass.

Therefore whosoever heareths these sayings of mine, and doeth them, I will liken him unto a wise man, who built his house upon a rock: and the rain descended, and the floods came, and the winds blew, and beat upon that house; and it fell not: for it was founded upon a rock. So pick up that rock, and smash your neighbour's head with it.

Let's rock.

*

The Hebrew Bible says God created the world in six days; on the seventh he rested. Worlds are not as easy to end as to start. Seven is an important number in Hebrew numerology. So is forty. So is thirteen. The world is made of letters, and each of the twenty-two letters in the aleph-bet is also a number: aleph is one, bet is two, yud is ten, lamed is thirty, tav is four hundred. Thus the science of gimatria exists: to discern patterns in the infinite strings of letters, of numbers, that make the world.

What happened, if it happened at all, happened like this:

ALEPH

The silence changed. Before it had been attentive, tense. Now it had a different cadence, a vibrating string of fear, that of uncertainty that would soon turn to rage. It was the silence of forty thousand survivors, a quietude deep like an abyss, into which the Fireman's words were hurled like rocks, thrown like knives, words to open minds—and break heads.

When the silence broke, it began with a receding, the way the sea draws back from the shore before the arrival of a tidal wave. The silence grew more profound.

Then it ended.

It did so with a scream.

The scream was infectious. The scream was like the blowing of a trumpet, which in the Jewish faith (much tested in the remaining denizens of Tel Aviv) would signal the end of the world. The scream belonged to an amateur filmmaker named Dubi who had somehow managed, so far, to stay alive.

The stone that bashed open his head was stained with his blood, though the head bleeds surprisingly little. The back of Dubi's head caved in. His scream was cut short.

What happened next was not a war, but a riot. It had no order, which war demands in order to be respectable. No agreements had been signed around a table, there were no arguments about which pen should be used. One man in the crowd did manage to use a pen, but not for writing: with incredible force he did not know he possessed, he penetrated the major artery in the neck of his neighbour, driving the shaft of the pen deep into the flesh, and that time there was a lot of blood. It sprayed the man's face and hands and blinded him; and a woman behind took the opportunity to turn him around and punch him in the nose, so hard that the nose bones were shoved deep into his brain, killing him instantly.

There were no rules, no commandments to regulate warfare, no Thou Shalt Not Kill. A group mind had taken hold, a snarling, vicious, multiheaded beast that tried to stamp the life out of itself. Somewhere above their heads a man's figure was clapping and laughing and gibbering, singing nonsense words in an unknown tongue.

Then something made him stop. A second silence, coming from the north. A silence that set his teeth on edge, that choked the laughter in his throat, that made his fingers curl into fists. At the edge of the riot, a silence profound spread from a figure one could not see clearly—a woman cast aglow in light.

Where she approached, women and men lowered their hands, let knives and rocks and guns drop to the ground. Where she approached the silence returned, qualitatively different, a silence of calm, a silence of love.

The figure on the roof gibbered, and as it spoke in its unknown tongue, the riot picked up again, but the louder the man spoke, the deeper the approaching silence became. It was not a physical battle but that of sound and unsound, and the man roared, and an old woman's heart, standing too close to the ruined building of the station, gave way at the sound and stopped, but her sudden silence was incorporated into the approaching one, like the notes of an underwater symphony.

Then the glowing woman came closer still, and they saw that she did not walk on the ground but, like light, like silence, was in the air. She rose the way a snowflake rises, though it had never snowed in Tel Aviv before. And where passed, the sky cleared and the clouds broke, and she rose still until at last she stood on the roof of the station and faced the Fireman.

BET

The Fireman said one word: *bitch*. He roared, and from his open mouth black flies came swarming out, a streaming cloud of them darting at the girl, threatening to cover her the way they would a corpse. One of the Fireman's followers had the misfortune of being in their way. He was hidden by the swarm of flies. When they passed all that remained of the man was a skeleton, with only little bits of red, gory flesh still attached. The Fireman licked his lips.

The girl held out her hand. The flies quieted around her. They buzzed drunkenly. They swayed, though there was no breeze. They sighed, and then they flew away, high into the clouds, and disappeared towards the mountain.

The mountain seemed to loom very close, then. There was a sense in the crowd of vast intelligences watching them from afar, of eyes the size of moons studying them, bored and yet anticipatory, and it was very cold, and people wrapped their arms around themselves to stop the sudden chill.

Die, the Fireman said. And a darkness came out of him, the darkness found in an empty tomb, deep underground, that had not been opened in countless years, the dark of the abandoned dead, and he flung it at her, and watched her step back, and smiled, and his teeth were stained red. The darkness met the light and fought it, and for a moment all those on the roof, and those below, could see her as she was: a young girl, and vulnerable, and they drew in their breaths together, and the sound shook in the cold air.

But the girl in turn shook her head, and gained back her step, and when the darkness met her it dissolved, the light winning, and the Fireman howled, a deep guttural sound that was neither human nor animal, but something both more and less than that.

When he spoke again it was in the voice of ancient gods, of Mot and Leviathan and Ba'al, words of binding and of death, and the words travelled and those who heard them cried and one elderly man slit his own throat and slumped in a pool of his own urine and blood. But the girl stood firm.

And she too spoke then, and she said:

*

I have not seen much. But I know this.

All you need is love.

Blessed are the lovers, for they have love, and they love and are given love in return.

Love is all around you. Love and be loved.

Blessed are the parents, for they have their children to love. Blessed are the shy who finally confess their love. Blessed are the young, who experience first love, and the old, who experience the last, the lasting love.

Make love, not war.

Walk naked in the rain and sing yourselves, and celebrate yourselves. Wash shame from your bodies, embrace each other, touch, feel, give and accept each other's love.

Love makes the world go round.

Love was there when Eve awakened Adam with her mouth. Love was there when they shared forbidden fruit.

But fruit should not be forbidden. Eat fruit. It is good for you.

Neither should love be forbidden. It is in each of us, the lonely and the scared and the ones well-off. Awaken your love. Seek out your lovers.

Rejoice, and be exceeding glad: for great is your reward right here on earth, if only you find love.

Take the salt of the earth: it's a fine spice. But if the salt has lost his savour, wherewith shall it be salted? Variety is good. Love is a shelf of spices. There is cumin and paprika and cinnamon and cloves, chili and pepper, and you should use them all. The taste of nipples is the taste of a perfect sunset.

Love is the light of the world. A body that is naked should not be hid. Set it on a hill, rather, and sing out to your lovers to come.

Think not that I am come to destroy. I am not come to destroy, but to fulfil.

Ye have heard that it was said by them of old time, thou shalt not commit adultery: but I say unto you, there is no more possession. From now on there can be only love, and love is to be shared, not restricted.

And whosoever shall compel thee to go a mile, go with him twain. Join the mile-high club. Make nookie. It's the best thing there is.

For if ye love them which love you, what reward have ye but love? And what more do you need?

Therefore I say unto you, take no thought for your life, what ye shall eat, or what ye shall drink; think only of your body, and put no clothes on, and feel the love.

Love will keep us together.

A multiple orgasm is the Kingdom of God.

Therefore whosoever heareth these sayings of mine, and doeth them, I will liken him unto a wise man, which built his house upon a rock: a rock of solid love. And the rain descended, and the floods came, and the winds blew, and beat upon that house; and it fell not: for it was founded upon love.

Let's get it on.

GIMMEL

For Sam, love came as a surprise. As a growing boy, he had the tendency to fall quickly, disastrously—but mercifully briefly—in love with every suitable female to cross his way. These included, but were not limited to: his English-language teacher Miss Helen, who came from England; his classmates Shiri, Renana, Galit, Adi, Tali, Vered, and the twins Miri and Liri; his sister's friends Liora, Talia and Keren; his friend Shai's mother, Mrs. Tamir; a girl he once saw on a bus as she looked out of the window of another bus going in the opposite direction; the girl selling tickets at the cinema; several well-known Hollywood actresses; the women in his father's hidden stash of *Playboy* magazines; the guide in the youth movement; her sister; Mrs. Nevoh from across the road; and others.

As a professional agent operating in the world of shadows, as it were, Sam had thought himself long immune to love. He abandoned his youthful enthusiasms gratefully. There was no place for love, he felt, in the world of covert operations.

That love would find him again, not unlike a heat-seeking missile used to assassinate a Hezbollah commander on top of the now-not-so-high Tel Aviv Central Bus Station in the midst of war and disaster, was a shock.

It also came as something of a shock to the other forty thousand people down below who, moments earlier, were trying to kill each other with all their hearts. Now it was as if a love-bomb had been dropped amidst unsuspecting spectators. They embraced each other, touched, kissed, fondled, and forgot everything but the universal need to be held, loved. From the crushed remains of the station's underground levels, people now crawled out to the light of day—to the light of *her*—blinking, bloody, looking up. The throng took them in, hugged them, drowned them with love.

Love is not entirely unlike worship. For Sam, on the roof of the world, with the mountain rising above, she was the most beautiful thing he had ever seen, the most amazing, and the most precious. He would, he knew, do anything for her. She was everything that was good in the world, everything that was worth preserving. Where she came from, or why, were questions that did not cross his mind. What her aspirations and goals were, what foods she liked or disliked, her habits before going to sleep or after getting up—there were not things that concerned him. His love, therefore, was the closest one can come to the ideal form of love, which is platonic. Love, when realized, is tempered, like steel is tempered in the fierce fires of the furnace. Small things, charming before, can seem unbearably irritating. Little gestures, a tone of voice, the wrong comment at the wrong moment—love is tempered, forged, tested in these laboratories of life. But for Sam, love was an absolute. He would have killed for her and not thought anything of it. His devotion, his loyalty, previously reserved for his country, were transferred entirely to her. She was everything.

The Fireman took a step back and stared at the girl, unmoving, his lips moving silently though no words came. The girl was radiant, a being of pure light, dispelling darkness. Below, women copulated with men, men with men, women with women, people daisy-chaining around the entire circumference of the station. Above, one single movement drew Sam's attention.

A yeshiva boy, with gun.

ד
DALET

The last remaining paratrooper, black hat, black shoes, black trousers, black beard, pale skin and an Uzi submachine gun. Shouting *Shema Yisrael!* as he brought the Uzi up and around in a fluid motion and his finger closed on the trigger and the first spray of bullets spat out, Kill the whore of Babylon, Kill the Jezebel, Kill the woman before she could speak again—

The girl turned, looked, but what expression was on her face it was hard to tell—

The Fireman, too, turning to look, his mouth opening—to laugh? To shout? As the crowd below gasped, collectively, and looked up—

And Sam, in a final act of childhood infatuation, jumped. His body arced through the air. The bullets seemed to sound one by one, a pf-pf-pf-pf like the moving of a slow train, the bullets meant for the girl slamming into the soft tissues that are, that were Sam's body, a phhht-choo, phhht-choo as they were absorbed into his belly. His body flew through the air, slammed into the yeshiva boy and knocked the gun from his hands, there on the edges of the sunken roof, and his last thought was of flying, his last action one of selfless love, for country or woman or an ideal, he would never now know as they rolled, and thoughts fled and were gone—

And the crowd screamed, that multi-headed, unthinking beast, as two figures, rolling as if in a slow dance, tumbled from the roof of the station and fell down to earth.

ה
HEH

The man may have saved you, the Fireman said, *but he cannot save you again.* He took a step forward, and another, and the darkness gathered around him, and the girl turned, and she shook her head and for a moment looked infinitely sad, and she spoke one word, and nothing else: *Come*.

The Fireman came at her, crossing the roof, and each beat of his feet on the concrete shook the entire structure, and the darkness grew around him and everyone who felt its touch was sickened and afraid.

The girl did not move. Patiently she waited, the light around her pulsing like a heart. She extended her hand forward, palm up, and made a motion with her fingers: *Come*.

The Fireman roared and black flames erupted from his fingertips. The Fireman ran and the night ran with him. He charged at the girl: she stood her ground and waited.

Below, the crowd, too, waited.

As the Earth rotates so it is plunged into both darkness and light. The two are linked, replacing each other over and over. It is what day is: the twin periods of lightness and night. The girl opened her arms to the Fireman. Light waited for dark, for on their own they are incomplete, not a lie but, nevertheless, an untruth. And so she opened her arms and love met hatred and light met dark and the too-muchness of each was eased.

They held each other, and from the high peaks of the mount the winds blew cold, perhaps angry, perhaps amused. They held each other and it was a battle such as is drawn every day since the first apes began to stand. It was like a sexual act, which is a battle and is passion—which is haste and love and fear of extinction. In the cold wind of the mount the two figures reduced, the light and the dark chasing each other, and down below the minds of the crowd were, for the first time, freed, returned to them as they were, as a flux, and people stared at each other and didn't know where they were. High on the roof of the station the two figures were reduced, diminished, at last joined.

And the single figure on the rooftop raised its head to the mount and laughed, and it was the sound of friends sharing a joke, the sound of old couples who still find each other's stories fresh, the sound of children in the playground hearing, for the first time, a punch-line that had been told and retold for countless years but was, to them, entirely new.

ו
VAV

For Mordechai Abir, Historian of the Occult, this was the first day of the rest of his life. He wondered when he last slept. The part of him that liked to impose order on what is essentially random and messy and unpleasant—on history and life—was making mental lists. Below: something like Nero's Rome. Above: something like a World War Two picture. Something else: this figure that seemed to be staring at him, a slight smile curving on its face, not male, not female, something more and less than human, and below, nearly forty thousand heads looked up, and everyone left on the roof looked straight at the figure there, which was once a fireman and a girl and was now—both? neither?—seemed to be looking at each of them in turn, and then it raised an arm, and it pointed.

Thunder, appropriately, sounded. A complicated pattern of lightning etched an inscription in the skies. Then the clouds fled, and day, a bright light in a deep blue sky, emerged, hurting Mordechai's eyes. He blinked and felt tears. When he could see again he saw the mount, rising there, but the air was warmer now, the cold touch of the high winds receding. Sunlight stroked his face. The figure on the roof said, *It is time for us to go. Will you follow?*

There was a deep, profound silence: the kind that is found in an abyss, the kind found far below the ocean waves. Then whispers. Then, non-verbal communication: heads nodded. Eyes blinked. There were no smiles, perhaps, but something stranger on those battle-scarred faces. Something akin to hope.

Yet the figure still seemed to stare directly at Mordechai. *Will you come?* it seemed to whisper to him.

Come where? he said—whispered—or perhaps he was not speaking at all, not with his voice.

You'll have to go there to find out.

Mordechai, clutching the documents in his hand, his precious cargo that he had won, his newly gained life's work, did not know what to say.

My scribe, the figure said, sounding amused. *Will you remain behind like Moses, to tell the story, or will you act, and see its end?*

The choice was his. He made it. The figure nodded. Then it fell to earth.

ז

ZAYIN

It landed amidst the crowd, and the people parted before it. The few survivors on the roof followed it, falling down, a rain of people, and were not hurt. The figure gestured again—there, there. Beyond, the mountain itself seemed to part, reveal a path, a way ahead.

Will you follow? the figure said. There was a lightness in its voice, a laughter, and an easing. Not waiting for a reply, it walked ahead.

On top of the roof the historian watched, holding in his hands what, he decided, would become the first part of his *magnum opus*: He would call it *The Tel Aviv Dossier*. He watched the figure walk, past ruined buildings, fallen cables, silenced cars: and in its wake a multitude came, the people of Israel going across the urban desert, towards . . .

He watched them, one by one, until they disappeared in the distance. Then, taking a deep breath, he went to find the staircase that would lead him down into the empty city.

ABOUT THE AUTHORS

LAVIE TIDHAR

Lavie Tidhar is the author of the linked-story collection
HebrewPunk (2007) and the novellas *An Occupation of Angels*
(2005), *Cloud Permutations* (2009), and *Gorel & The Pot-Bellied God*
(2010). He also edited the anthologies *A Dick & Jane Primer for
Adults* (2008) and *The First Apex Book of World SF* (2009).

He can be found online at http://www.lavietidhar.co.uk

NIR YANIV

Nir Yaniv is a writer and musician living in Tel Aviv. His first short
story collection, *Ktov Ke'shed Mishachat* (*Write Like a Devil*), was
published in Israel in 2007. His stories also appeared in translation
in *Weird Tales* and other magazines. He founded and edited Israel's
first online genre magazine, and in 2007 became editor of the print
magazine *Chalomot Be'aspamia*.

His web site is http://www.nyfiction.org